Forever Romances

A Distant Call

Patricia Dunaway

Forever Romances

is an imprint of
Guideposts Associates, Inc.
Carmel, NY 10512

For Patricia Moore
My very special friend, my "Nurse Patt"

Copyright © 1985 by Patti Dunaway

All rights reserved. Written permission must be secured from the publisher to use or reproduce any part of this book, except for brief quotations in critical reviews or articles.

This Guideposts edition is published by special arrangement with Thomas Nelson Communications.

Printed in the United States of America.

Scripture quotations are from the King James Version of the Bible.

All of the characters and events in this book are fictitious. Any resemblance to actual persons, living or dead, or to actual events is purely coincidental.

ISBN 0-8407-7367-6

Chapter One

The emergency room at the community hospital of Marvin, Texas, was like the hospital itself, small and modestly equipped. Johnny Allen made a conscious effort to block the pain in his leg. Lying flat on his back on the examining table, he forced himself to systematically scan the glass-enclosed shelves with their precisely arranged instruments, the rows of medications, the tall green oxygen tanks, the—it was no good. He closed his eyes and inhaled deeply, concentrating now on the strange mix of odors—the sharp antiseptic smell of hospital, the earthy aroma of his shirt and the remnants of his Levi's. He must have fallen in a *big* pile.

The nurse, whose name badge read Mrs. Juanita Patterson, RN, came bustling in, carrying a tray of white wrapped bundles. "It'll only be another minute. The doctor's coming real soon now." Her broad Texas drawl was touched with just a hint of her Mexican heritage, and she was a tall pleasant looking woman with salt and pepper hair and fine dark eyes.

Johnny figured she must be somewhere between fifty and sixty, but she wore her years of good Tex-Mex cooking well. "Thanks," he said, almost managing to hide the flash of pain, "Mrs.—"

The smile that looked at home there lit her face. "Just call me Nurse Patt. All the kids do," she said. "Sorry I had to cut up your britches like that." She put the tray of instruments on the metal cart, then bent to retrieve the right leg of a fairly new pair of Levi's. "Phew! You're sure not too careful where you sit. Where'n the world did....?"

She stopped as another woman pushed open the swinging doors and came hurrying in. For a moment Johnny wasn't conscious of having to suppress the pain in his leg; it just faded into the back of his head. She looked about his age, twenty-six or so, with soft-looking wavy blonde hair that surely must reach her waist when it wasn't knotted up, as it was now. And her wide gray eyes were so clear he was sure she'd never told a lie in her life. Her up-tilted nose wrinkled slightly as she drew near him and the offending Levi's.

Glancing at the chart she held, she said, "Hello, Mr. Allen."

"Hello," he said, thinking that though every inch looked perfect, she couldn't be much over five feet tall.

Suddenly aware of his close scrutiny, she drew herself up and put the chart in Nurse Patt's hands, ignoring her amused expression. "Let's get a look at that leg, Mr. Allen," she said seriously.

"Call me Johnny."

She didn't reply as she bent to examine the damage to his right leg. Her hands were small, her touch light. No nail polish, Johnny noted; he hated polish.

"We'll have to get some pictures, of course, but it looks like a fairly straightforward break of the tibia. However there is a great deal of bruised tissue." Gently she touched the area close to the break.

"Um hmm." Johnny winced in spite of himself and struggled to concentrate on the fact that she wore a pale pink shirtwaist dress, which was knee length and a big improvement over most nurses' uniforms. For such a small woman, she had absolutely spectacular legs.

"Patt," she said, interrupting his thoughts, "will you call Casey and ask him to get over here as soon as possible? We need to get Mr. Allen into X-ray right away."

Mrs. Patterson was already moving out of the room, but she stopped as Johnny said, "Ah...can you tell me when I might see the doctor?"

The young woman in front of him frowned. "Mr. Allen, I *am* the doctor."

He chuckled. "You don't look like any doctor I've ever seen. You look like a—"

"Yes, well," she broke in hastily, as though she was afraid of what he might say, "I most certainly am."

"What's your name then, Doc, and where's your white coat and stethoscope?"

The teasing note in his voice was really obvious now. She lifted her slightly pointed chin. "My name is Dr. Rachel McGeary and my coat is in the laundry...because Jill Mayberry threw up on me a few minutes ago." Meeting his mischievous eyes, she shrugged, and tried hard to suppress a smile as she said firmly, "Patt, see to that call, please."

Johnny waved to the older woman as she mock-saluted and left the room. "You *sound* like a doctor," he said. "But as for looking like a doctor, that's another matter. An angel, maybe."

"Mr. Allen—"

"Johnny."

"Mr. Allen," she repeated, her tone polite and professional, "I assure you I am the doctor in charge. Are you in much pain?"

"Nothing I can't handle." He put both hands behind his head and watched her. "I've never had a doctor who was beautiful before. They've always been men, and looked like the back wheels of bad luck. I think I'm going to like this."

Rachel held his gaze, chin still high, as she deftly unwrapped a couple of the sterile bundles Nurse Patt had left. "Hang on, Mr. Allen, and we'll get this cleaned up."

Johnny felt a tiny tremor of apprehension in his belly. "Now's the time to bite the bullet, I take it."

She stopped for a couple of seconds, then said gravely, "Don't worry; I won't hurt you. I'm told I have good hands."

As she began cleaning the ugly wound, Johnny closed his eyes. Her touch was still light, but somehow an authority—was that the exact word he wanted?—also came through. And he had the conviction that although she was the neatest, prettiest little woman he'd seen in a month of Sundays, she sure had told the truth: she was a doctor. Just as he was about to ask how she'd come to choose medicine, the door was pushed open. Johnny looked up, expecting to see Nurse Patt.

Instead, his eyes met the blue ones of a big man whose barrel-chested body seemed to make the room shrink. In a voice to match the body, he said, "Rachel, darlin', I need to talk to you about Lana Beth. You know we're gonna have to come to some kind of decision, and soon." He nodded perfunctorily at Johnny, who felt the tension in her hands immediately as the man spoke.

"I'm about through here, Dr. Burleigh, so if you'd like we can step outside and discuss the Duvall case."

"Oh, I reckon we've discussed it enough, Rachel. I told Lana Beth we'd let her know this evening—"

"Mr. Allen, will you excuse us?" Rachel asked, interrupting Burleigh.

Johnny watched with interest as she took the older doctor's arm and began to steer him toward the door with all the skill of a champion bulldogger. "Sure, *Doctor* McGeary," he said, not missing the little look she flashed him.

Alone for a moment, he took another deep breath, trying to will away the pain, wishing he'd told her how bad it was. He clenched his fist and pounded once, twice on the cool leather of the table. If only he hadn't tried to land on his feet to dazzle the crowd. Reckless, Mama would say; Johnny's my reckless one. They'd have to put a cast on the thing and he'd be on crutches for a couple of months. No more rodeo for him, for a while at least. He'd been coming to Marvin every weekend now through the summer, because a friend from way back was the ag teacher at Marvin High. He was also in charge of the rodeos held at the small FFA arena. Johnny had enjoyed them all...until today.

This time when Johnny heard the door whoosh open, it was Nurse Patt. With her eyes narrowed just like Mama's, she said, "Tell Dr. McGeary how bad it hurts, and stop that flirting for ten seconds so she'll hear you. She'll give you something. You don't have to play macho man for her. In fact, I can guarantee she'll like you better if you don't."

Johnny smiled ruefully. "You guarantee it, huh?"

"Sure do. Okay, let's get you out of the rest of those dirty duds and into one of our designer gowns." With a wicked little grin, she dangled the open-back garment.

"I think I'll pass," he said, scowling.

"Oh, no, you won't. Can you get your shirt off, or did you hurt your arm, too?" Purposefully she moved toward him, and Johnny had the sinking feeling there was no escape.

"I can manage." Johnny tugged angrily at the pearl snaps of his cream colored cowboy shirt. "And I can manage what's left of my new Levi's, too."

"Oh, no you won't" she said again. "Never been in a hospital before, have you?" He shook his head, scowling at his helplessness. "I can always tell." She watched him struggle to remove his shirt, then turned slightly away while he unbuttoned his pants. "Well, you'll learn."

"Learn what?" he ground out, trying to ease his legs from the jeans.

She smiled as she helped him, a beatific, infuriating smile. "Son, to me you're more a patient than a man, so relax."

"Not likely," Johnny muttered, shrugging into the indecent little gown and clutching the sheet she gave him. Somehow its cool white expanse reassured him as he lay back, almost exhausted, to wait for Dr. Rachel McGeary to return.

Rachel took a deep breath. *Count to ten*, Dad always used to say; *losing your temper just makes points for the other side*. Her mouth curved in a determined bright little smile as she sized up her adversary, and not for the first time, either. Dr. Anson Burleigh was old enough to be her father, a fact he used to his advantage with dismaying frequency.

How many times had he run his fingers through that thick, lively white hair that put the Colonel's to shame, fixed his blue eyes on her, and said with a disarming grin, "Now darlin', surely you didn't mean you wanted to—" And before she knew it her idea or proposal was scuttled, shoved aside, forgotten. Though she'd only been working at Marvin Community Hospital a little over a year, the pattern was set, and they both knew it.

But Rachel didn't give up easily on anything, especially not something that mattered. "Dr. Burleigh," she began, only to have his surprisingly small and finely shaped hand pat her shoulder gently.

"Now Rachel, I've told you a hundred times, there's no need for that kind of formality between us." She drew away slightly as he tucked a stray tendril of hair behind her ear, much as he would for his own daughter. "Why, I can remember when your daddy told us your mama was expecting you."

She ignored this often repeated reminiscence and zeroed in on his first statement. "That's just it, Dr. Burleigh, I really do feel there's a need for, well, I don't think formality is exactly the right word. Maybe..." She hesitated, then plunged in. "Maybe respect is a better word to express what I'm talking about. After all, I *am* a doctor, and I feel it would be best if you called me Dr. McGeary in front of my patients, not darlin'!"

"Why, Rachel, I sure wish I'd known you felt that way." He smiled. "I'm really sorry."

You old goat, she fumed inwardly; *you knew, and*

you're not the least bit sorry! Aloud she said coolly, "All right, Dr. Burleigh."

"Now *Dr.* McGeary," he said, his tone faintly mocking, "about Lana Beth."

"What about her?" asked Rachel, eyes narrowed.

"Well, when I talked to her mama today she was put out that we really aren't doing much, and I've about decided—"

"You've about decided? Lana Beth is *my* patient!"

He held up a placating hand. "Now dar...Doctor, of course she is." The words were spoken in as pleasant a Texas drawl as Nurse Patt's at her most relaxed, and there was a smile on his face. But the look in his blue eyes was sharp and watchful. "I'm just afraid that young woman is not far from serious trouble, maybe even kidney surgery."

"But Dr. Burleigh, you can't possibly be even thinking of that at this point!" Rachel was dismayed to hear her normally low, almost contralto voice come close to squeaking.

"I think it's about time someone did something to relieve that poor child's suffering."

Rachel drew herself up as tall as possible. "I'm not against getting another opinion, especially since we obviously haven't got the total picture with Lana Beth yet. But I also feel that I'm capable of—"

He interrupted her, saying, "Of course you're capable, but I've already made some inquiries, and there'll be a bed available at St. Joe's on Monday."

"You did that without consulting me?"

"What else could I do? Her mama was pretty close to hysterical, her husband's worried sick...her mama and daddy have been patients of mine for a long, long time, you know." His tone implied that Lana Beth had been his patient too, until Rachel had set up practice in Marvin. "Anyway, I just picked up the phone and made one little old call, and they both felt better right off."

"Did Lana Beth agree to this?"

"Why, sure she did," he said, giving her one of his famous—at least among his female patients—smiles. "The problems we're having aren't with you and me, darlin'," he said, lapsing easily into familiarity again. "The main problem is this—" he waved a deprecating hand, "—this old hospital. Outlived its usefulness, it has."

"That's not true, and you know it!"

"Now Rachel, I don't know any such of a thing. You just have your loyalty to your daddy all mixed up with things."

"No, Dr. Burleigh, that's not so." This was the first time he'd come out and said, in so many words, what she'd heard him imply too many times in the past year. "I can't deny that I'm proud that Dad had the foresight to build this hospital. I also believe the need for it is even greater in Marvin now than it was then."

"But Dr. McGeary, we both know there are a great many cases...such as Lana Beth's," Burleigh said softly, "that we simply are not equipped to diagnose."

"That may be true, but there are others—"

"And we want what's best for the people of Marvin, I'm sure you'll agree."

"Of course. But what we don't agree on is this hospital. I've seen this discussion coming and have wanted to say something. Now is as good a time as any. Whatever it takes to keep Marvin Community Hospital open, I'll do," Rachel said flatly. "Now I have to get back to my patient, Dr. Burleigh."

"Surely. We'll discuss this again, I trust."

He didn't move as she strode purposefully to the double doors of the emergency room, but Rachel was sure he was watching her. Under her breath she murmured, "Count on it, Burleigh!" As she reentered the room she took advantage of the moment provided by a burst of laughter from both Nurse Patt and her new patient to observe Johnny Allen.

Six feet two, brown eyes, dark, wavy auburn hair

...an extremely good looking man with a probable broken tibia. Her observation made her react a bit more coolly than she otherwise would have when he asked, "Well, Doc, is the lady going to be all right? What's wrong with her, anyway?"

"Mr. Allen, we haven't been able to make a diagnosis yet, which is too bad. She's a good friend of mine." She looked at his eyes keenly and thought two things. They were a little darker than cinnamon, and there was some shocky looking pain in them. "Patt, get me one hundred milligrams of demerol. You're in pain, aren't you, Mr. Allen?"

"Some," he admitted reluctantly.

"Is it all in your leg?"

"Uh..."

"Come on, the truth." Rachel's voice was quiet, but firm.

"Well, I'm beginning to think that renegade took a swipe at a rib," he said ruefully.

Rachel made a notation on his chart and moved close to the edge of the examining table. "I see."

She pulled the gown up to his chin and for the first time in her professional life had trouble concentrating. Johnny Allen was staring up at the ceiling overhead as though the whole thing was commonplace. But his smooth, broad chest belied that, for his breathing was quick and shallow. Rachel felt for his pulse. After a moment or two she said, "Your heart is racing, Mr. Allen. Does it hurt when you breathe?"

"Some. But don't worry about my heart racing. That has nothing to do with what happened earlier this evening." His eyes met hers, and their gaze held for a moment.

"Tell me what did happen." Efficiently but gently she proceeded to check his chest, noting the darkening bruise where she suspected the cracked rib, noting also that he had the trim, strong body of a serious athlete.

Masking his little wince as she took the syringe from

Nurse Patt and smoothly injected his arm, he said, "A bronc decided he resented my riding him and almost stomped the stuffing out of me."

"A bronc?" Rachel frowned as she drew the sheet up. "You're a goat-roper, then."

He made a face at the term. "No, at least not a full time goat-roper. Weekends I like to do a little rodeoing, though, and a friend of mine runs a good show here. Ever go out to the FFA arena?"

"No," Rachel admitted, "I haven't."

"Too bad. We might have met under better circumstances if you had."

"Hm." Rachel took out her ophthalmoscope and leaned close, peering into his left eye, then his right. "Everything looks okay in there. I take it the bronc didn't stomp your head."

"Yeah." He laughed softly. "You smell nice."

She drew back hastily and assumed that cool, chin-up attitude. "Mr. Allen, are you feeling any better after the injection I gave you?"

"Oh, I'm feeling great. And it's not all due to the shot, either." His grin was lopsided and a little silly; the injection had, indeed, begun to take effect.

Rachel turned to the obviously fascinated, uncharacteristically quiet Juanita Patterson. "Would you mind checking to see if Casey has arrived yet, please?"

"Right. It's a cinch you don't need me here," she teased as she breezed out.

"I like her," said Johnny, his words soft and a bit slurred.

"So do I." Rachel leaned against the wall, not knowing why she wanted to know more about this man. "If you aren't a cowboy, what do you do for a living?"

"I'm a petroleum geologist for Shell."

"Oh, really?" Rachel said, impressed. "Do you like your job?"

"Very much, since I got through college."

"Where did you go?"

"Rice University." Not at all disturbed by her curiosity, he answered willingly.

"Oh, well, I can see why you wanted out. Rice isn't the easiest place to get into, or out of, even if you're a scholar."

"Which I'm not. But it was plain as the pretty little nose on your face that I couldn't get where I wanted to go without a degree, couldn't have the things I wanted."

"What kind of things...?" Rachel trailed off, aware she'd probably crossed the line of propriety with that question.

But he answered as though it were the most natural thing in the world that she should be interested in him. He spoke of his family, of his father's job as an oil field worker, his own early decision to go even further in an oil-related career. He finished by saying, "From the time I was eighteen I knew what I wanted and did what I had to do to get it."

"Determination," Rachel mused softly.

"I've got lots." He grinned suddenly. "How about you?"

"I—" She halted, realizing again she'd been reacting to him in quite an unprofessional way. "Casey, the X-ray technician, is probably here. I'll go and see—"

"Don't go."

His quiet words shook her a little. "I...I beg your pardon?"

"Nurse Patt will come and tell you when Casey comes, so don't go. I feel better when you're in the room." She smiled uncertainly, but made no move to go, and he said, "Tell me how you decided to become a doctor."

An honest, straightforward question. How could she resist that? "I just always knew it was what I wanted," she said simply. "My father was a doctor, a very good one."

"Like you." His brown eyes were not as bright now;

they were dulled somewhat by pain and medication. But they held hers steadily. "I remember reading that some people are natural healers. They walk in, say a few positive things, touch the patients...and they feel better. You're like that."

For a moment she was silent; then she said slowly, "Thank you, Mr. Allen. I'd certainly like to think you were right."

"Oh, I'm right." He closed his eyes, and she took his wrist, feeling for his pulse. "Doc, you're going to have to get Nurse Patt to do that. Every time you try, it makes my heart beat twice as fast."

She frowned, her tone severe as she said, "Mr. Allen, you're a tease and a flirt. Cut it out and let me do my job."

"Me? A flirt?" He chuckled. "Doc, that may be your most accurate diagnosis of the day!"

"Well, cut it out," she repeated. "I need to—" She was interrupted by Nurse Patt, who told her Casey was ready and waiting in X-ray.

Half an hour later Johnny was comfortably settled in room 14. He looked up expectantly as Rachel entered, and his roguish smile lit his face. "What's the verdict, Doc?"

"Just what we expected, a clean break of the right tibia, and a cracked rib on the left side. I'm going to tape your chest now, but we'll have to wait until the swelling goes down before I can cast the leg. And we have to get that cut on your leg healed up a bit first, so you won't have problems inside the cast."

"How long will that take?"

"A couple of days at the most."

"An exciting weekend in Marvin Community Hospital, huh?"

"Not what you had planned, I imagine."

"Are you on duty all weekend?" he asked suddenly.

"As a matter of fact, I am on call."

"And you won't pass me on to that Burleigh guy?"

"Of course not," she answered, frowning a little. "You're my patient, Mr. Allen."

"Johnny, call me Johnny. I place my life in your hands, Doc. Say, you aren't by any chance a heart specialist, are you?"

"No, I'm a general practitioner." She stopped, then added slowly, "Why did you ask if I'm a heart specialist?"

"Because of the effect you have on my heart."

Realizing he was teasing again, she slapped her bundle of tape and instruments on the bedside table. "Get ready, Mr. Allen, because I'm going to do a very thorough job of taping your ribs. And it might even slow you down a tad!"

"I doubt it, Doc. I doubt it." His grin was so knowing and impudent that she considered taping him too tightly, but she was interrupted by Nurse Patt who came hurrying in.

"I'll do that, Dr. McGeary," she said, taking the scissors and tape from her. "Mrs. Brown in 10 is having another spasm, and I told her you'd be right there."

"Thanks, Patt." She glanced at Johnny Allen just before she turned and left. "As for you, behave yourself. I'll be back."

"Can I count on that?"

She didn't answer, just set off in the fast walk she had perfected as an intern. Never run to a patient no matter how urgent the call, or you might keel over when you get there. And Johnny Allen wasn't going anywhere. She didn't try to analyze her feelings, but that thought made her step even livelier.

Chapter Two

As she drove to the hospital in her vintage Volkswagen, Rachel realized that unlike a lot of people, she liked Monday mornings. It seemed as though each day had a rhythm peculiarly its own, and after her rather busy Sundays, Monday presented a welcome slower pace.

Beyond her hospital duties Rachel's Sundays included working with preschoolers and playing the piano at her church. Whoever said that Sunday was a day of rest must have meant the Sabbath, because the Lord's day in Marvin, Texas, was a day of worship, and worship with preschoolers sometimes got pretty strenuous.

She mentally listed what lay ahead. Though Lana Beth was still a baffling puzzle, Mrs. Brown could be discharged and taken home by her eager family, and the swelling in Johnny Allen's leg had most likely subsided enough by now to allow her to cast it.

Johnny Allen. Rachel wheeled into the hospital parking lot with the careless bravado most VW drivers show, braked, and cut the noisy little engine.

For a moment she rested her chin on her arm, staring out at the clear early-morning brightness of the August day. It was quite warm, but she knew fall was coming. She loved all the seasons, but fall was her favorite. It was then that she felt more alive, more full of life than at any other time of year.

Idly she wondered if Johnny Allen liked the fall, and if she'd ever see him again once he was released. At the somehow bothersome thought that perhaps she wouldn't, she grabbed her bag and hurriedly pushed open the door of her car, lightly grazing the dark green sports car parked beside her. Dismayed, she saw the three-inch scratch that marred the door. She'd have to find its owner and confess.

Rachel looked down, inspecting her pale peach dress. It was made in her favorite shirtwaist style and belted tightly at the waist with a muted blue and peach and cream Madras plaid cummerbund.

She chewed her lip for a moment, thinking she shouldn't have given in to the small prompting of vanity, that she should have worn more comfortable shoes. Rachel took delight in her twenty-one-inch waist and size-five-quad feet, but the high-heeled, backless straw sandals she wore weren't appropriate for a hard day's work. But she also knew they made her legs look good, and she liked feeling tall.

With a sigh at her own frivolous weakness, she reached into the back seat and drew out the comfortable cork clogs, resolving to put them on at the first hint of fatigue...or maybe the second. She was greeted at the door by a wide-eyed, agitated little LPN whose first name, Willow, seemed to fit her exactly. "Slow down, Willow, say it slowly."

"Oh, Dr. McGeary, I don't know what to do. He won't take his medication. He says it's not doing any good, that he's going to die anyway and he won't—" As her short, bright, curly red hair bounced, she looked like Orphan Annie with eyes.

Rachel put an arm around Willow's shoulders as they walked down the hall, deliberately measuring her steps, willing the girl to calm down. "I gather Walt Kovalcik was admitted last night after I went home." Wordlessly Willow nodded. "And Dr. Burleigh hasn't come in yet, and Nurse Patt's busy and told *you* to tend to Walt."

Willow nodded again, blue eyes wide. "You're so smart, Dr. McGeary."

"Not smart, Willow, I just know how things go around here." They were at the nurse's station now, and Rachel glanced at the partially opened door to Johnny Allen's room. Casually she asked, "Have you checked on 14 yet?"

"You mean Mr. Allen?" A sly little smile turned up the corners of Willow's carefully painted rosebud mouth. "Sure, first thing. Isn't he the best looking man you ever laid eyes on?"

To herself Rachel said, *Possibly*. Aloud she said severely, "I didn't mean his looks, Willow. Has he had routine morning care, his breakfast, have you checked his vitals—"

"Well, sure," Willow said, aggrieved. "And he asked twice when you'd be in today."

"He did?" Rachel firmly quelled the little glad rush she felt. "I'm sure he just wants to know if I can put the cast on so he can leave."

"I don't think so." Willow allowed herself a huge sigh as she brought out the charts for Rachel. "I think he thinks I'm too young and you're just right."

"Willow! I'm Mr. Allen's doctor, nothing more."

"Sure," the girl muttered just loud enough for Rachel to hear, "and I'm Dolly Parton." A woeful downward look at the ironing board front of her white uniform accompanied another huge sigh.

Rachel let both the sigh and the remark go by as she studied the charts. Her conscience made her put Johnny Allen's last; after all, he wasn't in any medical distress. It was Lana Beth Duvall's room she entered first.

Though Lana Beth's face brightened when Rachel pushed open the door and walked in, somehow the sight of that expectant, hopeful smile wrenched Rachel's heart. If only she could find the cause of the puzzling symptoms that plagued her lifelong friend.

"Rachel!" she exclaimed, then got mock serious. "That is, Dr. McGeary, I presume?" Her black eyes, now smudged beneath with the shadows of her illness, were warm. Tall and thin, dark-haired and crackling with energy when she was well, she had made a perfect foil for the petite blonde Rachel as the two went from first grade through high school graduation together.

Their paths had diverged after that, Rachel's to college and Lana Beth's to marriage the summer after graduation. She had three children now, and a husband who loved her but was thoroughly perplexed about her continued illness. Rachel looked at the chart.

"How are you feeling today, Lana Beth?"

She held up her hands. "My wrists ache, but not as bad as my knees. I need a good long walk." Her grin was wry. "But my bottle isn't full, so I don't suppose you'll unhook me and let me take a hike!"

Rachel looked at the offending bottle and made a notation: *Urine output low*, keeping her face carefully neutral. "Appetite?"

"None," she admitted softly. "Nothing sounds good. And I'm so tired." Her eyes filled with tears. "Rachel, I'm so tired of being tired. My kids need me—"

"Your mother still staying with them?"

Lana Beth nodded, the tears spilling slowly over. She rubbed them away like a child, with the knuckles of her fist. "But Rich has about had it."

Rachel's little grimace was one of sympathy. Lana Beth's mother was a nice lady, but as Aunt Lyddy would say, she'd drive a saint crazy. "Lana Beth, Dr. Burleigh tells me you've got an appointment with a kidney specialist he recommended."

"Oh, Rachel, I hope you won't think I don't trust you, but Rich and Mom insisted—"

With a couple of little steps Rachel was close enough to grasp her friend's hand tightly. "I don't think that at all. I understand, but promise me you won't make any hasty decisions."

Bleakly she said, "I'd never do anything...or let them, unless you agreed."

"There's something we're missing, and I'm going to keep trying to put the pieces together until we find it."

"I know you will. But Rich has begun to say...." she faltered.

"What?" asked Rachel softly.

"That if there was something wrong with me you'd be able to find it, that I've just gotten to be a hypochondriac," she whispered. "And I'm not."

"Of course you're not! And we're going to find out what's causing you to be sick." Rachel sounded far more positive than she actually felt. "We've got to get you in shape for my wedding."

Lana Beth's big eyes got bigger. "Rachel! Are you trying to tell me something?"

"No! I just meant...well, I'm not getting any younger, you know, and you've got three kids already, and we're the same age, and—"

For a moment Lana Beth's thin face had that old impish look. "Willow kept rattling on about a good-looking patient in 14. How about it, Dr. McGeary, is he husband material?"

Flustered, wondering why she'd even brought up the subject of a wedding, Rachel scowled. "He's just a patient with a broken leg."

"Well, old friend, just don't let him break your heart. One of these days you've got to let me stand up for you at your wedding like you did for me." Her eyes got wistful at the memory.

Rachel squeezed her hand once more. "We'll beat this, Lana Beth. And I'll be there this afternoon when you check in at St. Joseph's."

Lana Beth nodded. The prospect of facing another barrage of tests drained her face. "We have to do something, Rachel."

"I know. I'll see you later." Rachel flashed a smile as she left that was prompted more by love than hope. She checked her watch, seeing as she headed toward number 14 that it was almost ten o'clock.

He was reading. "Doc! I've been waiting for you." His eyes swept over her, and an appreciative smile lit them. The white hospital gown emphasized the lean brownness of his face, and as he marked the book Rachel noticed two things. It was poetry, Robert Frost; and his hands were large, but well-shaped, with long fingers and clean, cared-for nails.

Chin lifted, eyes on his chart now, pen poised, she said in her most professional tone, "Did you have a restful night, Mr. Allen?"

"Are you kidding? I'm used to a king-sized waterbed. It's a good thing this skinny bed has sides on it, or I'd have flung myself into the next county."

"Restless night," she said in a monotone as she noted it on his chart. The sudden image of Johnny Allen in a king-sized waterbed filled her mind. "And your leg? Having any pain?"

"More like discomfort." He was resting on one elbow, and his gaze swept from her high-knotted hair to her shoes. "Speaking of legs, yours are terrific."

"Please be serious, Mr. Allen—"

"I was never more serious in my life. You've got great legs," he said solemnly, then broke into a smile. "Don't tell me you don't like to hear it."

"I..." She hesitated, then smiled back. "Okay, I won't. But I'm here to talk about your leg, not mine."

He shrugged and raised his eyebrows expressively. "Going to put a cast on it today?"

"Probably. Let's take a look." She pulled the sheet back carefully, wondering again at her lack of objectivity, of professional detachment. It only took a moment to see that the leg was much improved. "You must live right, Mr. Allen."

"I try hard." His face grew sober, and he drawled, "Ma'am, I don't drink or smoke or chew, and I don't go with girls that do."

Rachel laughed outright. "Be that as it may, the cuts are healing nicely and I think it'll be fine to go ahead and cast it."

"That's good."

"Anxious to leave us, hm?" she said, hearing a light, teasing tone in her own voice.

"This bed and the hospital food, definitely yes. You, no. But I have plans."

Not quite able to bring herself to ask what he meant, Rachel murmured something about getting things ready to cast his leg and left.

A little later he watched as she carefully wrapped and plastered his leg from knee to toes. "You're really good at that."

Rachel had been concentrating but looked up with a twinkle as he spoke. "I considered going into orthopedic surgery, but they kept telling me I wasn't big enough or strong enough," she grinned.

"Well, you aren't exactly muscle-bound, but I'll bet you could do most anything you set your mind to."

She straightened, a little flustered but determined not to show it. "In a couple of weeks I'll be able to put a walking cast on. Or," she added quickly, "it might be more convenient for you to go to your doctor in Houston."

"You're my doctor now," he said firmly. "By the way, how's the woman you and that other doctor were discussing the other night?"

"No better." She finished the cast, smoothed it neatly, and began to gather up the assorted paraphernalia. "I'm going to go in this afternoon to meet her and her husband. She's being admitted at St. Joseph's Hospital."

Thoughtfully he asked, "You're going into Houston today?"

"Yes, I need to visit my aunt. Her name is Lydia, but most people call her Miz Mac. She's been a patient at St. Joseph's for a couple of weeks now."

"Is that so?" His brow was furrowed and he was gazing at her speculatively. "What kind of car do you drive?"

"A Volkswagen. Why?"

"Oh, just wondering. Is your aunt seriously ill?"

A bleak sadness clouded Rachel's gray eyes. "She has cancer. She's doing better, though, and I'm thankful for that."

"You care a lot about her, don't you? I can hear it in your voice," Johnny said quietly.

Rachel nodded. "She's really the only family I've got. When my folks died—"

"*Both* your mother and dad?" he interrupted with a frown. "How?"

"Dad owned his own small plane. He loved to fly, and Mom was learning...we never did know exactly why they crashed..." She said the words lightly, matter of factly; how many times had she repeated them?

"Poor kid. How old were you?"

The sympathy in his voice made Rachel's throat a little tight, which was silly. After all, they'd been gone for over sixteen years. "I was only ten, but sometimes even now I can't believe it happened."

"That's really rough. I come from a close family, and I can't imagine not having anyone."

Defensively Rachel protested, "I've got Miz Mac."

"Yeah, but—" he began.

"Mr. Allen, Miz Mac is no ordinary aunt. She was my dad's only sister, and she took me in as soon as the news about their accident came. She not only gave me a place to stay; she bought me pretty clothes, told me no when I needed it, and sent me to medical school."

He grinned. "No ordinary aunt for sure. I'm looking forward to meeting her. Say, would you please hand me my clothes? A buddy brought me some clean things when he dropped my car off." When Rachel stood speechless, he motioned toward the closet. "They're in there, unless you want to see how I navigate on this masterpiece you just engineered."

Rachel went over and brought back the blue plaid shirt and Levi's. "Just tell me one thing."

"What's that, Doc?"

"When exactly do you plan to meet my aunt?"

He gave her a lazy smile. "Oh, I figure if I sweet talk you a little you'll take me into Houston with you."

"You think so, hm?"

He nodded, his eyes holding hers. "What about it?"

"I—"

"I don't trust many people with my car."

"You mean you want *me* to drive you into the city in *your* car?"

"Sure. Wait'll you see it. I'll bet there aren't any more like it in the parking lot, probably not in the county."

A sudden sinking sensation hit Rachel's stomach. "Is it green?" He nodded. "A low-slung sports car?"

"A Porsche. With not a scratch on her, and she's twelve years old, too." The pride in his voice was unmistakable.

"There is now." Rachel's own voice was tiny.

"What?" His brow wrinkled in a puzzled frown.

"A scratch," she said meekly, backing out of the room. "I bumped it with my car door."

"What?" His face fell, and there was more pain in his expression than when she'd first seen him in emergency last Friday evening.

"I'll be glad to pay for it to be painted...and I'll be glad to drive you into Houston, Mr. Allen," Rachel said hastily from the doorway, hoping it would help.

It did, a little. He nodded weakly. "Is it a bad scratch?"

"No, not really," Rachel's voice came from the hallway. "It's hardly noticeable at all."

His moan was clearly audible, and Willow gave Rachel a questioning look as she passed. Rachel wondered what she'd let herself in for.

After gamely assuring her that the scratch wouldn't require more than a little touchup, Johnny carefully folded himself into the low seat on the passenger's side, his right leg straight out before him. He tried not to look anxious as Rachel adjusted the driver's seat, buckled herself in, started the powerful engine, and smiled brightly over at him.

"It can't be too different from mine," she said. "After all, it's just a glorified VW with extra zip." He winced as she backed out entirely too fast to suit him, then sped out of the parking lot with a discreet little roar. "Say, this is fun!"

"Yeah, fun," Johnny muttered as she wheeled around the corner and braked abruptly at the railroad tracks, because there was a freight train blocking their way.

"Well, it was your idea that I drive, you know," she needled him gently.

"Right." He watched the slow-moving, rhythmically clicking boxcars parade past. "Can you tell me why they laid out this town so that downtown Marvin is only two blocks long? On one end there's Highway 90, and on this end the tracks."

Rachel, almost hypnotized by the sluggishly moving cars, replied, "I don't have the slightest idea why they planned it this way. Maybe they didn't plan it at all. Maybe it just grew."

"Could be. But I'll bet with the hospital over here you get into trouble sometimes, don't you?"

"You're right. More than once ambulances have been held up. And there's a man, a pretty important man, I might add, who drove his pickup through the barriers because their timing is off."

"Got tired of waiting, I take it. Maybe he didn't have as pleasant company as I do."

She glanced at him briefly. "Look, it's almost through." As the caboose clicked past, she put the Porsche in gear smoothly and shot across. In the blink of an eye they were through the little town and heading south, toward Baytown.

Grudgingly he said, "You drive very well." After a moment's hesitation, he added, "Like a man."

Rachel frowned as she saw the speedometer had crept almost up to seventy, and slowed down. "Is that supposed to be a supreme compliment?"

"What do you mean?"

"Just that you sound as though only men drive well, that it's unusual for a woman to."

"Hey, I didn't mean to imply that."

Rachel thought... *Oh, didn't you?* but said only, "The fact is, I learned to drive when I was twelve. Lana Beth Duvall's daddy let us drive round and round their pasture in his old pickup. We had to keep the gear shift propped in with a forked stick." She smiled at the memory. "We messed up the dewberry bushes something awful, but we learned to drive."

"Well, you're doing great now."

"For a woman?" she asked. The smile on her own face faded as she saw the thoughtful look on his. "Mr. Allen—"

"If you drive my car, you call me Johnny," he said, sounding a little subdued.

"All right, Johnny." For a moment Rachel concentrated on the familiar golden rice stubble on either side of the straight highway, the flash of a red-winged blackbird, the brilliant, endless blue sky overhead. The windows were down, and the rushing air was hot but fresh. They were both silent for a few miles. Then, as she turned onto I-10 she said slowly, "We weren't really just talking about driving, were we?"

"No, I guess not." His gaze was speculative as he faced her, his arm draped on the back of her seat, touching her shoulders lightly. "It never even occurred to me that you might be a—"

"I just resent the fact that when men tell women they think like a man, or run their businesses like a man, or... *drive like a man*," she said slowly, emphasizing each word, "it's supposed to be a compliment."

"Well, aren't there things men do better than women and vice versa?"

"Surely, but don't you see, if I said, Johnny, you drive

like a woman, you wouldn't think of that famous race car driver...what's her name?"

"Janet Guthrie?"

"I think so. Anyway, you'd probably think of some female ding-a-ling who shouldn't drive anything but a three-wheeled bicycle, when the truth is there are some monumentally awful male drivers, too."

"I just never thought of it like that," Johnny admitted.

"I guess not," murmured Rachel. She suppressed a sigh, thinking she should have kept her opinions to herself.

His next words proved her wrong. "Say, Doc, would you like to go out for dinner tonight?"

"Sure," she said faintly. "I'd love to."

"Good. If you have time and wouldn't mind, could we stop off at my apartment so I can change?"

"I don't mind at all. Where is it?"

"Not far from St. Joseph's, as a matter of fact," he said as he put his head back on the seat, murmuring something about taking a catnap.

The vast network of oil refineries, chemical plants and storage facilities seemed to stretch endlessly as she drove the familiar road. Rachel glimpsed the San Jacinto Monument for a second, thought fleetingly of childhood picnics there, watched the procession of traffic coming and going—anything to keep from glancing at the man beside her.

She wasn't always successful, for her eyes seemed drawn to his fine profile. She wondered if his hair was as soft as it looked. And he had such long lashes. Why was it that little boys and even men so often had lashes that would make a woman weep with envy?

The third time she glanced over at him he caught her. He smiled, and she couldn't keep from smiling back. She was very much looking forward to the evening with him, even if he was a little...aggravating.

Chapter Three

Rachel had called from Marvin and told Miz Mac she was bringing a friend, and Lydia McGeary's appearance gave every indication that she had dressed especially in anticipation of meeting him. Her pale blue robe was new, her face was carefully made up, and she wore a turban the color of forget-me-nots.

She looked up as they entered the room and slipped her makeup mirror beneath the covers. "Rachel, I'm so glad to see you!" Her arms opened wide, and Rachel went straight into them.

Holding the thin body close, Rachel thought fleetingly of how just a year before Miz Mac weighed at least twenty-five pounds more than now; and she'd been slim, then. "You look wonderful, Aunt Lyddy. That color is good on you." Seating herself on the edge of the bed, she turned back to where Johnny stood balanced near the door. "This is Johnny Allen, a—"

"A patient of yours, by the look of him!" Her merry blue eyes still sparkled, despite the draining influence of the treatments which were, mercifully, finished yesterday. "How do you do, Johnny Allen? What do you think of my new headgear? A young woman came in earlier and taught me some of the neatest tricks you ever saw to cover up this bald noggin. Pretty clever, wouldn't you say?"

Rachel fought the sudden squeeze in her stomach. It was just like Miz Mac to wade right in and bring up the fact of her baldness.

"I think it looks terrific," said Johnny. He made his way over to the bed and took the hand she offered in both of his, no mean feat on crutches. "It matches your beautiful eyes."

Miz Mac shot a quick glance at her niece. "You'd better watch this one, Rachel. He looks like he could charm the birds out of the trees."

"Tell you what, Aunt Lyddy, you watch him for me. If I leave right now, I won't be but a couple of minutes late to meet Lana Beth and Rich." She looked from her aunt to Johnny, who still held her hand. "I don't know which one of you to tell to behave."

"Then just go on about your business and leave us to get acquainted," Miz Mac said tartly. As Rachel moved from the room she heard her aunt say, "Sit down and take a load off your feet...foot, young man. And tell me about yourself. Rachel doesn't often bring young men to meet me. You must be something special."

"The truth is, I conned her into bringing me."

Johnny's confession was the last thing Rachel heard as she slipped out, breaking into that fast walk of hers down the corridor, wishing she had on jogging shoes instead of the ridiculous high heels.

Watching Lana Beth's admission into the hospital was as difficult as Rachel had expected. The doctor, a fine specialist, seemed nice enough. But Rachel couldn't shake the feeling that he saw Lana Beth almost exclusively as a "kidney patient," not as a whole person. Most certainly not as a friend. But Rachel made it through the process, hoping she'd hidden every aspect of their relationship but the professional one.

Instead of returning to Miz Mac's room immediately she went to the hospital library to check on a thought in the back of her mind. An hour later she pushed open Miz Mac's door, amazed to see Johnny sitting on the bed and both of them laughing breathlessly.

Fists on hips, Rachel stood staring for a moment. "What in the world is going on?"

"We've had a nice visit," said Johnny. "Your aunt has told me all about you."

Rachel's own smile was weak. "*All* about me?"

Miz Mac nodded, her expression as mischievous as Johnny's. "I even told him about the time you and Elvia skipped school and went over to Liberty and—"

"Aunt Lydia!"

"She must really be mad," murmured Miz Mac to Johnny, who slipped off the bed and reached for his crutches. "She never calls me that."

"Oh, you know I'm not really mad," Rachel admitted. "But it certainly looks as though you two didn't have any trouble getting acquainted."

"Not a bit. I know some of his kinfolks from way back, and he likes flowers and you. What better recommendation does he need?"

Rachel eyed first her aunt, then Johnny. Miz Mac owned a flower shop in Marvin and had hit upon the idea of combining antiques with her business a few years back. This stroke of genius had resulted in a wonderfully successful blend and gave Miz Mac a chance to roam the Texas hill country to her heart's content, looking for the Texas primitives she had a passion for. Had it not been for the shop, their house would have overflowed long ago. Slowly she said, "Recommendation for what, Aunt Lyddy?"

A little smiled played at the corners of Miz Mac's mouth, which was lightly glossed with an impudent shade of watermelon today. "Oh, who knows, child, who knows?" She touched her intricately wrapped head and, satisfied the turban was still secure, added, "Where are y'all going out to dinner?"

Johnny said casually, "I thought maybe the Meridian."

Miz Mac's lips pursed in a silent whistle. "La de dah.

Trying to impress her, hm?"

He shrugged. "The thought had crossed my mind. Think that'll do it?"

"It might. But you never can tell with Rachel. Why, I've known her to be happy with the last piece of chicken that went over the fence, if it was fried crispy enough, that is." A little gleam shone in her eyes, and she seemed about to say something more when someone knocked, and a man stuck his head in the door. "Come on in, Stan Janek. Meet my niece Rachel and her friend Johnny Allen."

The man did as he was bidden, and Rachel observed him closely as everyone murmured polite greetings. He was tall, gray-haired, slim, and probably a decade older than her aunt, with whom he was obviously smitten. He treated her with such deferential courtesy Rachel was touched. She also wondered why her aunt hadn't mentioned him. "How did you two meet, Aunt Lyddy?"

Mr. Janek gave Miz Mac a quick glance, then answered for her. "I was a patient here too, until a couple of days ago. We met in the living room."

"Living room?" said Johnny, a quizzical look on his face.

"You tell him, Rachel," prompted Miz Mac.

"Well, both of these two could probably do it better than me," said Rachel. "The main thing I know is, it's worked wonders for you, Aunt Lyddy."

"Me, too," put in Stan Janek. "Lydia likes the joke times, but I like the video cassettes."

"Hey, whoa!" Johnny laughed. "Joke times, video cassettes, in the living room...that doesn't sound like my idea of a hospital."

"Actually, it's a radically new approach to treating cancer patients," agreed Rachel. "A Houston oncologist, Dr. John Stehlin, conceived the idea, and designed the section of this floor that Aunt Lyddy's talking about, the Living Room. It has reproductions of famous paintings on the walls, comfortable places to sit and read, and lots of books and magazines. And stereos and video cassette recorders."

"Sounds great," said Johnny.

"It is. Every time I went there, which was often, I came away feeling better, more up." Stan Janek glanced at Miz Mac. "Even if Lydia wasn't there."

She rolled her eyes. "Oh, Stan, you do go on. Anyway, Johnny, they encourage us to entertain ourselves, to laugh. That's scriptural, you know."

Johnny grinned. "A merry heart doeth good like a medicine," he quoted.

"Right!" Miz Mac looked at him with fresh interest. "You like proverbs, then?"

"Yep. And you like jokes?"

"Yep. We all have to tell one every time we get together in the living room. Heard any good ones lately?"

"Don't stop me if you've heard this one," said Johnny, that cocky grin still on his face as he launched into the latest joke making the rounds in Houston.

Miz Mac's laughter rang out. When she caught her breath she said, "Well, if you two are going out on the town, you'd better get going."

Johnny glanced at Rachel. "Maybe we had. I need to stop off at my place and change my clothes, remember?"

"All right." Rachel turned to her aunt. "If Mr. Janek will—"

"Stan is my given name," he interrupted gently.

Rachel smiled; he really seemed to be a gentleman in the best sense of the word. "Stan, then. Are you going to be staying longer?"

"If she'll let me." He gave a barely disguised look of adoration at Miz Mac.

"Of course you can stay, Stan. You ought to know how lonesome these rooms can be." She reached out and caught Rachel's hand, squeezed it, and let it go. "You two get on out of here. But before you go, I've got some mighty good news. Dr. Baker is letting me out of here tomorrow."

"Oh, Aunt Lyddy, that's wonderful! Why didn't you tell me?" asked Rachel.

"You were too busy doctoring, and I was too busy getting acquainted with this Texas primitive!" She glanced mischievously at Johnny, who returned the look.

Rachel kissed her aunt and laughed, but she was struck with the same anxiety she always felt when she went home without her.

In the elevator Johnny said quietly, "Don't worry about her. Mr. Janek has obviously taken a shine to her, and we'll be coming back for her tomorrow."

"*We* will?" She smiled up at him. "What is this *we* business?"

"Think it over. You're driving my car, so you'll have to take it home, which means you'll have to pick me up in it tomorrow." The elevator door opened, but he made no move to get out. "I sure hope you didn't think there were no strings attached to this deal, because there are."

The door closed, but she managed to press the button before it started up again. "I guess I can live with the arrangement," she said lightly.

Rachel had never actually wanted for anything in her life. Her father had made a comfortable living, and Miz Mac's home provided a pleasant gentility. But the sheer opulence of Johnny's condominium awed her, even subdued her as she sat in his living room while he changed clothes.

The room itself was so artfully, tastefully done she felt as though she ought to sit erectly with her legs crossed at the ankles like Miz Mac had taught her. The furniture was an outrageously expensive looking arrangement of deep, almost seductively curved cream linen that blended into the deep pile carpet of the same shade.

There were huge palms and ficus trees placed beside gleaming brass tables and a pair of stylized brass curlew birds that fascinated Rachel. The only other ornaments were a small wooden carving of a horse nipping at an invisible mosquito on his shoulder and a brass vase in the shape of a paper bag tied with twine, which held peach and gold gladioli spears.

She sat quietly, enjoying the spectacular sight of the Houston skyline against the backdrop of the lush green trees—Hermann Park.

"How do you like the view?" Johnny's question jolted her from her bemused state.

"It's beautiful." She waved a hand at the sumptuous room. "This whole place is...very impressive."

"We also have a concierge and valets, tennis courts, a great pool, and a fitness center—"

"Where you can lift weights?" broke in Rachel, thinking of his muscular, trim body.

He nodded, adding wryly, "And use the sauna and steam room to recuperate."

As he went to the floor-to-ceiling window, Rachel noticed he'd already gotten the hang of using the crutches. For a man, he moved with surprising grace. She bit her lip at the thought that she had just done what she'd accused him of—assuming men as a rule aren't graceful. "How long have you lived here?"

He swung around to face her. "About six months. Do you like it?" He now wore a pair of pale beige slacks—probably chosen because the legs were wide enough to accommodate the cast—and a dark brown Egyptian cotton shirt which fit his lean body snugly.

And no gold chains, Rachel was glad to see. A little hesitantly she said, "Why, yes, of course, who wouldn't?"

"When I was a kid growing up in Saratoga—"

"The Big Thicket," Rachel murmured.

He nodded. "Anyway, I had the best family God ever blessed a man with, but there weren't many extras."

She got up and went to stand beside him at the wide expanse of glass. "And you decided when you were able you'd live differently."

"Right. I drive a fine car, I live in an expensive, beautiful place, eat what I want. I have almost everything I ever wanted."

His last statement was accompanied by a sudden, intense meeting of their eyes. Rachel moved restlessly away. "We really should be going, shouldn't we?"

"Sure." He gave her a one-sided smile, his eyes thoughtful. Then he swung around, pivoting on one smooth-soled Italian loafer. The stiff leg with its white, sock-covered foot brushed the soft carpet. "Get my jacket please, if you don't mind?"

Rachel fingered the fine nubbly weave of the oyster linen all the way down the swift, noiseless elevator. As they emerged into the twilight she noticed that the air was a little cooler. She looked down at her dress. "Couldn't we go some place a little less elegant than the Meridian? I'm not really dressed for—"

"You look great to me."

"Thanks," said Rachel, "but I'd feel better if I had something different on."

"Hey, I'll be proud to have you on my arm." He was shrugging into the beautiful linen jacket, and she had to admit any woman would be proud to be seen with him.

She wanted to insist they go somewhere else, but his attitude was somehow overwhelming. She found she couldn't insist. Though she almost managed to stifle the feeling of being woefully underdressed, Rachel was immensely relieved when the evening drew to a close.

As they neared his door, laughter lurking in her voice, Rachel said, "I'll have you know I feel silly walking you to your door!"

"How do you think I felt, having you chauffeur me around all evening?"

"It was good for you," Rachel declared, laughing up

into his eyes. What she saw there made her throat tighten, and for a moment neither spoke. Then she said slowly, "I had a wonderful time, Johnny."

"That's supposed to be my line," he teased. "But you're right, it has been fun. I'll have to admit it was kind of hard, having you drive and open doors for me, but...." He trailed off. "It was great, the whole evening, and now that I've seen you behind the wheel I trust you with the car, really. You're a good driver. By the way, what time are you picking me up tomorrow?"

"Is ten all right? Aunt Lyddy will be ready to leave by seven in the morning, but I'm sure everything won't be cleared until after eleven."

He was gazing down, and his eyes seemed almost black in the discreet lighting of the hallway.

"Ten is great. I really like your aunt."

"She liked you, too. I could tell."

"Good." He was quiet for a moment, then said, "I'll take the day off. I've got it coming," he added quickly as he saw the beginning of a protest on her face. "I'll be waiting."

Rachel stood for a moment, feeling as he had that they were somehow in reversed positions and thinking briefly, *So this is how a man feels, trying to decide if now is the time to leave, if he should kiss her or not* ...she hoped the quick flush she felt at that thought didn't show in the dimness. "Good night, Johnny," she said softly.

She was all too aware that he watched her walk to the elevator, watched until she disappeared from view. What had he said...*I'll be waiting*.

Chapter Four

Lydia McGeary's garden was a lovely place to be almost any time. It was encircled by fine pecan trees and carefully tended by Miz Mac herself. The light, haunting fragrance of honeysuckle wafted on the still, warm air, and Rachel released a contented sigh. From early spring she enjoyed this garden, with the first appearance of the always welcome tulips and narcissus, on to each bright perennial. Even now, with summer waning, there was a glorious sunset splash of chrysanthemums and marigolds. She watched as Johnny and her aunt sparred with words, one the victor at one time, the other gleefully winning the next round.

Johnny had insisted they stop by Luke's and get ribs for lunch, and the afternoon slipped away pleasantly. Rachel wondered if Johnny was simply good with older people or if he really liked Aunt Lyddy a lot. After all, most people did. Mr. Janek had been visiting again today at the hospital, and Rachel believed he meant every word when he asked if he could visit her in Marvin as well.

Unconsciously Rachel sighed. Aunt Lyddy had sworn she never intended to marry, and Rachel, at twenty-six, had begun to wonder if her own life might end up much the same. That thought was interrupted as Johnny threw back his head and laughed, a warm, hearty sound in the late afternoon stillness.

He said, "So you told the man Rachel was your daughter after you also told him you'd never married and never intended to! And what did he say to that?"

Miz Mac tossed her elegantly turbanned head—today a luscious shade of watermelon that blended perfectly with her lipstick. "Nothing, and if he had asked any more silly questions I'd have asked him if he had nose trouble." She leaned back in her chaise, bright eyes fixed on Johnny. "You ask a lot of questions yourself, young man, but somehow I don't mind. Most of 'em seem to end up being about Rachel anyway," she added, daring him to deny it.

He didn't. "Interesting topic," he murmured, glancing at Rachel, who sat a little apart. His eyes took in the intricate patterns of the Seminole patchwork dress she wore. It was made of many pieces—red, yellow, jade and turquoise stripped with black—and their brilliance sparked her fairness beautifully. "But it seems to me that a question about Rachel is a question about you. Let's see, you two have been a dynamic duo for—"

"Sixteen years," supplied Rachel, "since I was ten. And we've done pretty well, I'd say." As she exchanged smiles with Miz Mac, her heart twisted at the realization of just how lonely she'd be without her. "Is there anything I can get for you, Aunt Lyddy?"

"Not a thing, but I feel like this young man owes me equal time. How about it, Johnny? Tell us about yourself."

Johnny locked his hands around his good knee. He wore a tight-fitting maroon knit shirt, khaki drill pants, and tan Topsiders. "Well, I was born in 1958, at home, Doc, without benefit of a physician," he began teasingly.

Rachel smiled back at him. "Midwife?"

He nodded. "She was old even then, but she's still alive."

"I'd like to meet her," said Rachel. "I could probably learn a lot."

"I'll introduce you, arrange lessons."

"Midwifery is back in vogue, I'll have you know. But continue with your life story, Mr. Allen."

"There's not a whole lot more. I grew up chasing after coon hounds at night, trying to get out of going to school in the daytime. It wasn't until I realized how poor we actually were that I decided if I wanted something better, school was the only way to get it."

"It's funny how kids don't know."

"What's that, Miz Mac?"

Miz Mac had a gentle, musing expression on her face, a faraway look in her bright blue eyes. "When I was a kid it seemed to me as though red beans and rice, fried potatoes and mustard greens was about the best meal a body could eat."

"You mean it's not?" Johnny asked.

"You know what I'm talking about," she said severely.

"Yeah, I do." Johnny was quiet for a moment, then added slowly, "My daddy roughnecked till I was fifteen, when he finally got to be a driller. That's still a mighty tough job, and he had to be away from home a lot. Mama pretty much kept things going. Now that's one tough woman. You'll see when you meet her, Rachel."

Rachel merely smiled, not wanting to ask when he thought such a meeting might occur. "Aunt Lyddy, hadn't we better be going inside? Pretty soon the mosquitos are going to find us."

"You're probably right. And Johnny's probably getting hungry again." She allowed Johnny to help her up. "Thank you," she said, looking up into his eyes. "Your mama taught you manners, I can see."

"Well, Ma'am," he drawled, "she sure tried."

"Tell me, son, is she a godly woman—a believer—or did she just think good manners were important?"

The quiet, direct question didn't seem to ruffle Johnny, though Rachel's face showed that it made her a bit uncomfortable, as though she thought the question too personal.

"She's all those things, my mama is. And—I accepted Christ when I was fifteen, Miz Mac."

"Good. It always seemed to me to be a waste of time for Rachel to go out with young men who didn't know the Lord. She's smart enough not to marry a man who isn't a Christian, but I don't think she ought to waste time even going with one."

He flashed a grin at Rachel, who just said again, faintly this time, "We really should be going inside."

As the three made their way in by the French doors facing the garden Miz Mac said, "Nonie left some fruit salad in the ice-box for me. Where are you two going for dinner?"

Johnny took up the rather pointed question immediately. "I thought maybe Guido's."

"Guido's?" asked Rachel incredulously. "You mean drive down to Galveston now?"

"Sure, why not?" Johnny stood aside as the two women went in. "You said you like to drive my car."

"And she loves seafood," came Miz Mac's muffled voice from inside the refrigerator door. "You two go on. I'm just as happy as if I had good sense. It's so good to be home again." She walked slowly, holding the cut glass bowl of fruit salad in front of her gingerly, as though she had to be very careful.

"But Aunt Lyddy, I don't want to leave you alone so soon—"

"Good grief, girl, I was in that hospital over two weeks, and being here in my own house *alone* is just what I do want!"

"But—"

"But me no buts. I can call Gemma, or Nonie, if I need anything, which I won't. You two go on and get out of my hair." She giggled suddenly and reached up to touch the watermelon turban. "Just a figure of speech. Anyway, go on."

"Are you sure?" Rachel came over and hugged her aunt, who allowed her to for a moment, then pushed her away.

"I'm sure. Now get yourself ready before this young man changes his mind."

As Rachel ran up the curving staircase she heard Johnny say, "There's no danger of that, Miz Mac. Where Rachel is concerned, my mind is already made up."

Now what did he mean by that? Rachel wondered, as she stood at the door of her room listening for a moment to the pleasant laughter that drifted up, the distant murmur of their conversation. *You haven't even known the man for a week...why does everything he says seem so important?* "Because it is," she murmured softly, accepting the fact and going to her closet.

She stood staring at the neatly arranged assortment of clothes in the freestanding wardrobe, and for the first time in a long time it seemed as though she had very few clothes. There were the plain, but pretty, pastel shirtwaist dresses she wore to work and a smattering of folksy-artsy things like the one she now wore. There were not many slacks or pants of any kind. She thought idly that Johnny Allen was probably the kind of man who liked a woman in Levi's.

After another look at the vivid patchwork dress she wore in the three-cornered mirror, she decided it would do. *If a woman is not a clotheshorse, she's just not*, she thought resolutely. At the well-lit dressing table mirror Rachel freshened her makeup. Before applying the rosy lip gloss, she went into the adjoining bath and thoughtfully brushed her teeth, grateful beyond words they were white and straight, even if it had cost over two thousand dollars and three years of her adolescence to make them that way.

Back at her dressing table she outlined her mouth lightly, and filled in with the pearly pink color. Her hair looked all right even to her own critical eye, but she felt an obscure need to brush it, so she took out the pins that bound it, bent her head low, and brushed it slowly, carefully.

Even from upside down the large, uncluttered room pleased Rachel. The walls might have looked white to a casual eye, but she had mixed the paint herself and knew it had the faintest blush of pink. There was nothing hung on this softly glowing surface but a heart shaped wreath of grapevine and wildflowers and the antique oak frames holding pictures of her mother and father—their forever-young faces turned to each other.

With a little half smile, she admitted the bed's headboard was a departure from her rather austere taste. It was hand-crafted, made of slender bentwillow...in the shape of a heart. A homely, beautiful thing that Miz Mac had dragged out of a dusty storeroom, and wheedled an old man into selling her for a shamefully low price even as he protested it had been his grandmother's.

Rachel pinned her hair up again, but more loosely than before. Then she splashed Laura Ashley cologne behind her knees—she didn't like scent around her face. Just as she picked up her bag and was about to leave, she heard her aunt's knock. "Come on in." She tried to steel herself against the shock of Aunt Lyddy's appearance. She was so pale, so thin, But Rachel smiled quite normally, even teasingly. "Did you come up to give me some motherly advice?"

"Do you need it?" she fired back.

"I might," Rachel admitted.

"You might, at that. He's got it, whatever it is. What are they calling it nowadays, anyway?" She patted the turban, as though she needed to make certain it was still there.

Rachel eyed her aunt for a moment, then said with a chuckle, "Yes, he's got it. And since I seem highly susceptible to *it*...maybe you'd better give me that advice!"

Miz Mac laughed. "Tell you what, Rachel. If my instincts are right—and how many times have I ever been wrong—you can trust that one." She paused, a smile still lurking in the corners of her mouth. "Not that his juices aren't cooking, they are. But I just have this feeling about him."

"So do I," murmured Rachel very quietly.

"Mm, hm, I thought so. Anyway, I didn't come up to give you advice about Johnny Allen. You're on your own there. I wanted to know if it'd be too much of an imposition to ask you to stop by the store, just to check on things. Nonie does a fine job, but—"

"Of course we will." With her arm around Aunt Lyddy's shoulders, Rachel recalled how broad and strong, how capable of holding up anything, those shoulders had been not so very long ago. "Are you going back downstairs?"

Miz Mac shook her head. "Think I'll lie down for a spell."

"If Nonie is still there I'll tell her to stop by," Rachel said as she walked her aunt to her own room down the hall.

"That'd be good." She allowed Rachel to pull back the bed covers but balked at being helped in. "I'm not an invalid, and I'm not your patient!"

"But you're my...my—" Rachel stopped; she often thought *mama* and felt the oddest assortment of feelings—betrayal of her own mother, whom she'd loved dearly, confusion because Aunt Lyddy had been everything to her. "A friend can help a friend, if the friend who needs help will let her," she said gently as she pulled the snowy sheets up.

"Sorry," murmured Miz Mac. "I guess I am a prickly pear. But I can't just give up—I won't!"

The quiet determination in her voice was more touching than tears ever would have been to Rachel. "Of course you won't give up." Rachel risked a kiss on the smooth cheek and was rewarded by a slight squeeze on her own shoulder.

"Have a good time, honey."

Rachel nodded her head thoughtfully. "Somehow I believe that's a foregone conclusion with Johnny Allen."

And it did start well. He was pleased to stop by Miz Mac's shop—a delightful, if somewhat crowded place not far from the hospital. Amid the sweet clutter of greenery and Texas primitives, Nonie Blanchard was twittering, still trying to take care of the myriad details that Miz Mac could have dispatched in short order. Nonie was an ultra-feminine little woman, the opposite of Lydia McGeary's tall, spare good looks.

"I just can't seem to get caught up," she said breathlessly to Rachel, patting her fading blonde curls after an introduction to Johnny. "How's Miz Mac doing, anyhow?"

"Better," was Rachel's automatic reply. "Glad to be home. Nonie, would it be imposing if I asked you to go by? We're going down to Galveston for dinner—"

"Oh, really? That sounds awfully romantic!" Nonie's brows rose expressively. "There's a full moon tonight, you know."

Rachel ignored that arch comment, even managed to ignore Johnny's little answering grin. "Yes. Well, I'd feel better if you dropped by to see her." Nonie had been a widow for not quite a year now, and Rachel knew how long her evenings got.

"You know I'd be happy to, Rachel. And I'll stay as long as she'll let me, not matter *how* late you two are."

Johnny allowed himself a small chuckle. "Now Miss Nonie, I wonder if you'd do me a favor?"

"Anything, Mr. Allen, anything."

Rachel suppressed a smile. It was an established fact that Nonie had been Rachel's Sunday school teacher for the duration of her junior high years. It was also a fact that she was as truehearted and pure as God made women. But there was that need to flirt...as there was in most southern women. And with a man like Johnny, the whole funny, endearing ritual was inevitable.

He gazed into her blue eyes and said softly, "I'd like to buy those pink roses." He gestured to the enormous bouquet in the cooler.

"*All* of them?" Nonie's eyes grew even wider.

"All of them. And I want you to make up a super something for Miz Mac, too." He glanced at Rachel. "Could you give me one rose now and send the rest with Miz Mac's bouquet?"

Rachel started to protest that the roses alone were going to cost him over one hundred dollars, then changed her mind. She loved pink roses.

Nonie, obviously totally captivated by Johnny, quickly brought the great fragrant armload of roses, and fluttering an eyelash, she swept one beauty out and gave it to him. She couldn't contain a sigh as he brought out his pocket knife, cut off the few remaining thorns and shortened the stem, then tucked it in front of Rachel's ear.

Again Rachel started to protest, but instead she left it there with a little smile. Is there a woman alive who doesn't know how pretty she looks with a rose in her hair?

They were soon on their way again, leaving a laughing, wide-eyed Nonie as Rachel conscientiously helped Johnny in the car, fixed his crutches firmly, and closed his door. Then feeling a delicious bubble of excitement, she expertly put the fine little car in gear and roared off into the waning twilight.

Guido's faces the Gulf of Mexico, and only the broad, busy Seawall Boulevard separates the restaurant's front yard from the crashing waves. Inside, the crisp air made them shiver after the sultry warmth of the evening. Johnny and Rachel relished their dinner.

A laughing, very persuasive young waiter came to take their dessert order. Rachel stuck a finger into her snug waistband. "Look, no more room! We had those unbelievable shrimp cocktails *plus* salads—and by the way, the house dressing was perfect—baked potatoes with enough toppings to make a meal all by themselves, and the grilled swordfish that tasted as though you caught it this afternoon." She looked to Johnny for confirmation, but he just smiled and nodded, his eyes on her, not the young waiter.

The enterprising young man merely shrugged his shoulder. "Listen, have the cheesecake or regret it for the rest of your life. You'll never eat better, I promise."

"Okay, okay," said Johnny. "We'll share a piece." As the boy triumphantly wrote it down he winked at Rachel. She missed it, however, for Johnny asked softly, "I hope you don't mind. Sharing, I mean. Some people do, I guess."

"No, I don't mind." She looked thoughtfully at him, thinking how attractive he was. He wore a silky shirt that was very near the color of his eyes, and in the subdued lighting of the restaurant she could see his watchful gaze was as intent as her own. "Johnny, I hope you didn't mind my aunt's questions too much."

"Mind? Why should I?" He reached over and put his hand over hers. "But I would mind it if there was no one to care about you, interrogate possible suitors, look out for you."

She frowned. "Why do men automatically assume a woman needs someone to look out for her?"

"Hey, don't drag out that stuff, because I don't buy it." He shook his head, and gave her hand a little squeeze. "I'm not even going to try and deny that women have gotten the short end of the stick in a lot of ways...which we won't go into right now. But in all this feminist upheaval I think something really important gets forgotten, or worse yet, shoved aside."

"What's that?" Rachel asked, thinking his earnestness was extremely endearing.

"That men depend on women for everything from their very coming into this old world to warmth and sanity and the kind of love that can only come from a woman," he finished softly.

"That's beautiful, Johnny." Her own voice was just as soft, but each was so finely tuned to the other they heard the words easily, even above the swirl of activity around them.

"It sure can be when it's right." He took a slow drink from his frosted water glass, studied the remaining crystals of ice as though they were diamonds, then added, "We can't get along without each other—men and women that is. It makes me sadder than I can say to see friends whose marriages have gone sour—both of them with everything to give, and neither giving it. If I can't be certain *my* marriage will be different, I won't try."

Rachel felt suddenly, unaccountably shaky. She was grateful when the jaunty young waiter came striding up with the biggest, best looking piece of cheesecake she'd ever seen.

As she and Johnny shared the creamy treat which lived up to its billing they laughed a great deal, both very much aware of the heightened intensity between them. Carefully Johnny insisted on feeding her the last bite from his own fork, Rachel marveling that she'd certainly never allowed that before. Even as a small girl she'd been particular about eating with her own initialed silver. But with Johnny it didn't seem to matter at all.

After Johnny paid the outrageous bill they walked out of the air-conditioned chill into the soft evening air. The breeze off the Gulf was brisk but not too stiff. The traffic had thinned, and even at Johnny's pace they were able to cross the street to the wide walkway that topped the seventeen-foot-high sea wall.

"Let's take a walk," Johnny said, smiling down at her.

"But your leg—"

"Look, the moon is rising, the water is as nice as I've ever seen it, and I'm with the most beautiful woman I've ever known. I'd be an idiot to waste all that just be-

49

cause my leg is broken. Come on."

"Just promise you'll tell me if you get tired," she murmured, putting her arm through his. *To make sure he's steady*, she told herself, then admitted she wanted to be close to him.

The water picked up the smooth silver of the moon, fragmenting the shimmer and scattering it over its nearly smooth surface. They walked in companionable quiet for a good distance. With only a few voices in the air, they heard the rumble of hoofbeats on the sand. Soon they saw a girl with flying hair ride by on a horse.

"I always wanted to do that—ride a horse on the beach," said Rachel.

"There's something I want to do that it seems like I always wanted, too." He turned to face her. "Maybe you'd better put your arm around me."

"Why? Have we walked too far? Your leg—" She slipped an arm around his waist, wondering if she was strong enough to hold him up if he should topple.

But he let the crutches fall and put both arms tightly around her. "It's not my leg, Rachel. The fact is, if I don't hold you close, right now, I might die."

She started to laugh, but suddenly his lips were on hers. She thought crazily that if she held on tight and he held on tight and kept kissing her, they *might* not fall....Breathless, she whispered, "Johnny, it's only been a few days, not long enough—"

For answer he hugged her even more tightly and kissed the top of her head. "Your hair smells like honeysuckle. When I was a boy it used to grow all around our house. There was always a rose bush round the house, too." He buried his face in her hair, inhaling its fragrance and that of the rose. "I used to think rose petals were the softest things in the world, but that was before I kissed you."

"Johnny, I—" She stopped as he kissed her again, deeply and for such a long sweet time she was dizzy.

When he drew away slightly, his breath was as quick as her own.

He tried to see her face, and they almost fell, laughter rising in them both. "As for its being too soon, I'd say it's long overdue. After all, it is our fifth date."

"Our fifth?" she echoed incredulously. "How do you figure that?"

"You came into my room on Saturday evening, and I gave you my banana pudding. Dinner together, right?" He grinned down at her, daring her to contradict. When she remained quiet, eyebrows raised, he said, "Casting my leg was so much fun that it definitely qualifies as a date to me. Then even if you did drive to Houston, we went to the Meridian that evening, and for sure you have to admit that was a date." She nodded and he rushed on, "Lunch today with your aunt, number four, and tonight. Haven't we had a good time tonight?"

She bent and picked up his crutches, carefully propping him up. "Yes, but I'm afraid things are happening too fast, Johnny, and it spooks me a little."

"Honey, I sure don't want to do that. But I feel—"

She interrupted him gently. "I'm well aware of what you feel, and I never said I didn't. But we should go slowly—give things a chance to develop."

"Why?" The question was quiet, but challenging.

"Because...."

"Look, Doc, I'll try to go slow. But I've got the very definite feeling that something has started between us that's really important, something I've been waiting for. And I don't want to take a chance on losing it."

Once again she linked her arm in his as they began to walk slowly back the way they'd come. "Neither do I. But Johnny, please don't rush it."

The sound of the waves filled the evening air in the silence that followed. Then he said, each word quiet and thoughtful, "I'll try, Rachel. I'll try."

Chapter Five

Rachel took a deep breath and smiled determinedly up at Anson Burleigh. "I just get the feeling there's something you're not telling me, Dr. Burleigh."

"Now darlin', whatever gave you that idea? Don't you trust me?"

His blue eyes were doleful, reproachful. Rachel steeled herself against them. "It's not that I don't trust you, Doctor." *Oh, isn't it?* a little inner voiced taunted. *Be straight, Rachel, even though you feel he isn't.* Aloud she said, "I just believe you want to close the hospital and would do...almost anything to see it done."

The reproach turned to hurt now, and it seemed real enough. "Rachel, you've got to know how much it pains me to think that you'd think I'd do something dishonest or unlawful—"

"I didn't mean to imply that! And I certainly don't mean to question your integrity."

Burleigh squeezed her shoulder—a kindly, expansive forgiveness replacing the pain on his craggy, handsome face. "Of course you didn't, darlin'; of course you didn't. I can remember how it was to be young and idealistic—and unrealistic to want something just because you want it. You're going to have to do some deep thinking about this place, though. I'm certain your daddy would agree with me if he were still alive." One last squeeze on her shoulder, then he ambled off down the hall, stopping to talk to the young nurse on duty.

For a long moment Rachel stood watching him. Then she slowly made her way to the emergency entrance and stood just outside the door, where the sultry breeze lifted the hair at her temples and the nape of her neck. She sighed. Statistics—cold hard facts filtered into her brain. She was all too aware that the average hospital stay was down to 3.5 days. There had been a grand total of 6.6 patients admitted last week. And then there were the patients like Lana Beth, who had to be taken to larger facilities. The creeping doubts came for the first time. Could Burleigh possibly be right? Were small hospitals like this one becoming an anachronism?

"Hi, Doc."

Rachel looked up, filled with gladness at the nearby sound of Johnny's voice. He swung easily, quickly over to where she stood, but the kiss he gave her missed her mouth. It was closer to a chaste chin kiss. She covered the little feeling of disappointment well as she said, "It's so good to see you! How did you get here?"

"Oh, I roped a buddy into bringing me. How're things going?" He stood looking down at her, taking in her silvery blue polished cotton shirtdress. It made her gray eyes look the same color.

"Pretty well." Rachel knew it was unreasonable of her to wonder why he hadn't asked to see her since they'd gone to Galveston. After all, it had been her idea not to rush things. He had called daily, and he knew she was free for the weekend after ten tonight. "How's the leg?" she asked with what she hoped was professional interest.

"Doing great. In fact, good enough that maybe you could check to see if we can put a walking cast on now."

"But it's only been two weeks, Johnny." For a moment that thought stunned her; somehow it seemed as though she'd known him forever. "Oh, we'll check it.

Have you always healed quickly?"

He swung through the door as she opened it and followed her down the hall. "I'm disgustingly healthy. I've hardly ever needed a doctor." She glanced back at him, caught the quick flash of his grin. "Until now, that is, and I find myself needing to see a certain doctor a lot."

She didn't trust herself to comment on that, even in the teasing way. And she soon discovered his leg was, indeed, healing well. So she yielded to his request that she put a walking cast on.

"Now can I drive?" he asked, surveying his leg.

"Sure. Where do you want to go?" She stood fairly close to where he sat with his legs dangling from the table.

His eyes, on a level with hers, looked steadily back. "You're not on call this weekend."

"No, I'm not."

"Would you like to go to Saratoga to meet my family? I called Mama and told her about you. Now they all want to meet you."

"What did you tell her about me?"

He must have heard the little flicker of anxiety in her tone, for he said offhandedly, "Oh, that you're a totally modern, liberated lady who—"

"You didn't!"

He grinned. "Nope, I didn't. And I'm not going to tell you what I did tell her either, except that I was sure they'd like you."

"I'd love to meet them. You have a sister at home named Dolly, and—" She was interrupted then by Willow, the young LPN, who was more wide-eyed and breathless than usual.

"Oh, Dr. McGeary, it's the Lindsey boy, and he's bleeding an awful lot, and his mama is—"

"Slow down, Willow. Where are they, and what happened?" Rachel seemed to have forgotten Johnny as she led Willow from the room. Johnny watched, a bit awed by her display of cool assurance.

Rachel, when she saw the young Lindseys and their five-year-old son Daryn, took a quick deep breath and lifted him carefully from his father's arms. Willow had been right. There was a lot of blood. "Come with me to the emergency room, and tell me exactly what happened." The boy was rigid with fear, perhaps pain, and emitting a steady, high-pitched wail.

The young father spoke first. "It just happened a few minutes ago...he was running, and I told him to stop and throw it down—"

"I've told him a million times not to do it—" Mrs. Lindsey was tall, a pretty blonde who looked wild-eyed now with shock and fear.

"Not to do what? Daryn, what happened?" asked Rachel. But when the child opened his mouth another little rush of bloody saliva spewed out.

"Mr. Lindsey, calm down and tell me what happened to Daryn." Rachel's own voice was calm and laced with command.

It had the desired effect. Mr. Lindsey said, "He was running in the yard and he had a stick in his hand and he fell and stuck it in his throat—" Evidently the awful picture struck him dumb again.

Comprehension dawned on Rachel. She took a tongue depressor from the nearby jar, laid a cool, firm hand on the child's shoulder, and said, "Open wide, Daryn, and say ahh, just like you always do for the doctor." Obediently the little boy opened his mouth, and Rachel peered in quickly before he could change his mind. What she saw reassured her. She removed the depressor and began to clean the little boy up, knowing if she got rid of some of the frightening amount of blood his parents would feel better. "He'll be fine." To Daryn she said with a smile, "Well, are you going to be a doctor when you grow up?"

He nodded, still not speaking. "I thought so," Rachel said gravely, "because you almost gave yourself a tonsillectomy tonight. Your mom and dad are right, you know. You should never run with anything in your hand—except maybe a football."

Weak with relief, the young Mr. Lindsey sagged against the wall beside the table. "I can't tell you how glad I am you were here, Dr. McGeary."

"Me, too," said his wife, whose color was beginning to return. She smiled tremulously at Rachel. "We've always gone to Dr. Burleigh, but—"

Rachel interrupted smoothly. "Dr. Burleigh is a fine man. He worked with my father, and I've known him for a long time. There, Daryn, you don't look like you spilled a bottle of ketchup on you anymore." She smiled at the young couple. "You can take him home now. He'll have a sore throat, but he'll be fine in a couple of days. Have him gargle with salt water if you can figure out how to teach him to gargle."

Daryn giggled and spoke for the first time that evening. "Gargle. That's a funny word."

"But it certainly isn't funny when you don't mind me, young man," his father said severely.

Rachel left then, knowing it wouldn't be the last time Daryn heard those words. Johnny was waiting, and it was almost ten o'clock. The thought of a whole weekend with him filled her with the most delightful mix of apprehension and anticipation. The paperwork for Daryn Lindsey wouldn't take too long.

However, it wasn't paperwork that kept Rachel late. Mrs. Harmon pulled out her IV again, and Rachel had to use all her persuasive powers before the elderly woman would allow the needle to be reinserted. When Rachel took a moment to suggest that Johnny wait for her at Miz Mac's, he gladly agreed. By the time she joined him there, it was after eleven, and they decided it would be best to postpone the trip to Saratoga until morning.

With Miz Mac asleep and Johnny settled in the bedroom next to hers, Rachel found she couldn't sleep, though she was very tired. His nearness was somehow strangely, deeply disturbing.

She stretched her toes as far as she could into the cool depths of the smooth white sheets. Her door was ajar, and she knew his was, too. *Oh, Lord*, she prayed silently, *help me control my thoughts—my unruly thoughts.*

Saturday dawned clear, hot, and bright—a perfect September day. Aunt Lyddy looked much better now and Rachel was convinced that was due mostly to her being home. When she assured them that she would be perfectly fine, Johnny and Rachel set off for Saratoga. As they turned north for Liberty and headed toward Moss Hill, he glanced over at her.

"Ever been to the Thicket?" When she shook her head he said, "I can't believe it! Aren't you aware that there are species of flora and fauna in the Thicket that aren't found anymore, *anyplace*, in the country?" Again she shook her head. "Why, the Thicket is a national treasure!"

"I believe you! I believe you!" Rachel laughed at his intensity. "And the people in the Thicket, are they a national treasure, too?"

His expression grew serious now. "Folks are different there. They think differently in some ways."

Rachel stared at him for a moment. There was something in his voice that puzzled her. Surely he wasn't ashamed of his family?

Almost as though he read her mind, he said, "I'm not ashamed of them, if that's what you're thinking. My daddy's people all came from Alabama, and settled in the Thicket during the Civil War. And Mama's always talking about Indian blood on her great-grandma's side, so her folks have been around for a long time, too."

"Sounds to me as though your family has a lot invested in the area," Rachel put in quietly. She gazed out at the tall, thin-trunked pine trees, the wildly lush undergrowth.

"That's absolutely true," he said, sounding gratified.

"Then how do you mean they're different?"

There was a thoughtful silence before he answered, "Well, backward is what some people might say. Old-fashioned or traditional would cover it if they were being kind."

It was the first time he'd been so serious, and Rachel missed his usual spontaneous gaiety. "Look, Johnny, I live with Aunt Lyddy, who feels furniture built anytime after the turn of the century is worthless. I value old things and old ways, myself."

He shook his head. "It's not a matter of things, or even ways. It's more like...like ideas."

"What kind of ideas?"

But he was either unwilling or unable to articulate his thoughts. "You'll see when you get there."

The remainder of the drive was rather quiet, with neither speaking much. The vague anxiety Rachel felt was heightened by Johnny's reluctance to speak further of his family. When they drove down the still, almost deserted main street of Saratoga and out again in record time, she refrained from commenting that Marvin was a thriving metropolis by comparison.

After a couple of miles they turned onto a narrow gravel road, and finally he pulled up in front of a low, rectangular brick house which seemed to be the long-popular—in Texas, at least—ranch style. The only attractive thing about it to Rachel was the woman who stood in the door, her hands extended in welcome.

She wasn't much taller than Rachel, perhaps five feet four or five, and her dark hair had only a few silver strands here and there. "Come on in," she said warmly. "I'm Johnny's mama."

"And I'm Rachel McGeary, Mrs. Allen."

"Call me Nadine or Deenie like everyone else does, please." She gently pulled Rachel into the spotless little living room, calling back to Johnny to hurry on in, broken leg or no.

Whatever Rachel had expected, it wasn't this. She looked around at the brown Naugahyde sofa, the matching formica-topped coffee table and end tables topped with identical orange ceramic lamps, the two precisely placed rust plaid chairs. Everything seemed new, but so much plastic dismayed her. She said with a little smile, "It's such a nice room, Mrs....Deenie."

"Jim, my husband, picked out everything. He's real proud of our home. Would you like to see the rest?"

"I...of course." Rachel had never really understood the reasoning behind showing people through your home, but she wasn't about to say no. They made a little circuit of the house, ending in the kitchen.

"Oh," breathed Rachel thankfully, "What a beautiful kitchen!"

"You think so?" said Deenie. "Jim keeps after me to...to modernize it, but I like it."

It was a lovely room, far different in a lot of ways from the others. It spanned the back of the house except for the end bedroom and was as warmly welcoming as Deenie Allen herself. "I hope you don't change it, I like it, too," said Rachel, her eyes delighting in all she saw.

The cabinets were made of some fine grained wood, perhaps cherry, Rachel thought, and above them the bounty of a dedicated canner glowed like jewels. Green beans, corn, tomatoes, peaches, pears, beets, and more kinds of pickles than she could easily name were arranged in pleasing color patterns on top of the cabinets. A large bay window at the sink was filled with healthy green plants. An old crockery churn, filled with sunflowers, sat behind the dining table, which was well-used, round, and solid oak with intricately carved claw feet. Deenie motioned for Rachel to sit down and turned to hug Johnny, who'd come up quietly behind her and was watching the two of them.

"Johnny, you didn't tell any stories about her. She's every bit as pretty as you said!" She hugged him again, and looked up into his face. "Is your leg better? Want some coffee?"

He kissed her cheek, then let her go and went over to sit by Rachel at the table. "Yes to both questions, Mama.

What time's Daddy coming in for lunch now?"

"The same—twelve straight up. I swan, I thought it'd kill him to work regular hours, but he's still alive and on the job." She walked quickly to the cabinet and took out three cups. "I can sit a minute, but dinner's not quite ready, and you know how he gets if it's late." She poured coffee from a graceful hammered aluminum pot on the stove and sat down opposite the two of them, her brown eyes going from one to the other as though she were trying to decide if they went well together.

James Earl Allen came through the kitchen door a little while later—two minutes past twelve to be exact. He went straight to Deenie, who stood at the stove dishing up the meal. He put his arms around her waist and kissed her neck beneath her hair. When he turned around to face them, Rachel rose and took a couple of steps toward him, her hand extended.

"Mr. Allen, I'm Rachel McGeary."

He took her hand and didn't let it go. His was rough and calloused, but he'd obviously scrubbed at the traces of his job before he came home. "Glad to meet you, Rachel. Just call me Jim." His hair was the color of Johnny's and his eyes the same rich shade of brown. They appraised her frankly from head to toe. "I've always preferred dark-haired women, like my Deenie, here, but you could almost change my mind." He glanced over at Johnny. "You didn't tell us she could stand in for an angel, son."

"Now that you mention it, Dad, I believe I drew that same conclusion myself. But I ought to finish introducing her." He took a deep breath and said, "This is *Dr*. Rachel McGeary."

Jim Allen's expression changed subtly as he let her hand go. "Is that a fact. How come you never mentioned that, Johnny?"

Johnny shrugged. "Never thought of it, I guess."

Rachel thought she heard something puzzling in his tone but didn't stop to figure it out. "My daddy was a doctor, and since there weren't any sons to follow in his footsteps, I did," she said lightly.

"I think it's wonderful that she's a doctor. Dolly will certainly be interested," Deenie said, ignoring the quick frown that appeared on her husband's face as he went to the sink, scrubbed his hands, and splashed water on his face. She swiftly got a towel and placed it in his waiting hand.

He was a ruggedly handsome man, thought Rachel as she helped Deenie get the food on the table. Johnny's looks were similar, but somehow fined down. The two men conversed casually as the women put the meal out. It was much like other country meals she'd enjoyed: chicken fried steak with cream gravy and mashed potatoes, black-eyed peas, corn on the cob, mustard greens, a platter of sliced tomatoes, and quartered white onions in vinegar and water, heavily peppered and salted. There was also a huge chocolate-frosted cake on the drainboard. She was glad she didn't have to work this afternoon. A meal like this one tended to stupefy her. Obviously not Jim Allen, whose face bore a look of pleased anticipation.

"You're in for a treat," he said now to Rachel. "My Deenie's the best cook in these parts, and that's saying some."

Faintly Rachel murmured, "I believe you. This looks more like dinner than lunch."

Johnny chuckled, seating himself to his father's right. "I've heard Daddy say often enough that when people start calling the picture of the Lord's Supper, 'The Lord's Dinner,' then he might call dinner lunch."

Rachel placed the steaming, fragrant bowl of black-eyed peas on the table, sat by Johnny, and smiled in capitulation. "Then I'll say this is the best-looking dinner I've seen in—"

"In a month of Sundays?" supplied Jim. He waited for Deenie to seat herself, then lowered his head. He had a fine, deep voice, and his dignified prayer fairly rolled out, in a surprising contrast to his folksy, easygoing manner. "Oh, Father, we thank Thee for this bountiful table Thou has prepared for us. Bless it to the nourishment of our bodies and us, Thy faithful servants, to Thy service. Be with us, and most especially with our honored guest. In His holy name I pray, Amen."

Johnny had taken Rachel's hand, and as he lifted his head and gave her a little wink, he also squeezed her hand before releasing it.

"Look at that, will you, holding hands right at the dinner table. Give him an inch and he'll take a mile, girl." Jim cut his meat, a piece of steak the size of his hand, into six precise pieces, then looked up at his wife. "Hon, you forgot to pour my tea." Deenie immediately rose, came to his side, and poured his glass full of iced tea. "And while you're up, would you get me a couple more ice cubes?" She went to the refrigerator and brought back more ice, asking if Rachel or Johnny wanted more.

Wordlessly Rachel shook her head, watching as this little routine was repeated several times during the course of the meal. She found herself exasperated with Deenie for jumping up at his slightest word while her own food grew cold.

The two men finished eating and at Jim's suggestion went into the living room. Rachel ventured a timid statement. "Jim sure seems crazy about you." A little half smile was Deenie's answer as she took the last bite of meat from her plate and began scraping the dishes.

"That's a fact. He has been since he first laid eyes on me, to hear him tell it. We met at his baptism. He was a sight to see, I'll tell you, nineteen years old and so good looking." She got a dreamy, faraway look in her dark eyes. "When he came up out of the water, it fair took my breath away. He was as handsome as Johnny is now."

"He's still an attractive man," murmured Rachel. "But he does seem to, well, he expects a lot out of you...."

Deenie stopped stacking plates and faced Rachel. "I know what you're thinking—that he takes advantage of me. Well, you may be right. But that's the way things are in the Thicket. A man's home is his kingdom."

"That doesn't bother you?"

She shook her head. "Most of the time, no. Now, there are some occasions I have to really work hard to figure out how to get around some things, like with Dolly."

"How old is Dolly, anyway? I don't remember if Johnny told me, only that she's just finished high school."

An almost fiercely proud look crept onto Deenie's face. "Eighteen last month and bright as a new penny, even smarter than Johnny was at that age. She's bound and determined to go on to school, and I'm just as bound to see that she does."

"You mean to college."

Deenie nodded. "She wants to be a nurse. But he says a girl has no business—" She broke off, her fine, full lips a bit thin now.

"Her father," said Rachel thoughtfully, remembering the look on Jim Allen's face when Deenie had told him she was a doctor. Again she wondered why Johnny hadn't told them earlier.

Just then they heard Jim call out, "Deenie, Babe, bring me and Johnny some more iced tea, will you?"

Rachel had no intention of saying anything more on the subject at that moment, but Deenie said quietly, "Look, Rachel, I wait on him because he's my man and I love him more than I ever could tell you. He's a good man, has always provided well for us all. He could have gone on permanent disability a while back after he was hurt in that accident on the rig over past High Island, but instead he took a job down at the filling station. He hates it like poison, let me tell you. My Jim's just not the kind of man to sit around all day."

The woman's dark eyes were filled with emotion as Rachel stared into them. "I think it's marvelous that you still care so much about each other, after all these years. How long have you been married?"

"Twenty-nine years in December," Deenie said, moving toward the refrigerator for ice to put in the clean, tall glasses she'd set out.

Before Rachel could comment on that, a girl with long dark hair burst through the back door. She was tall, probably five eight or so, and slender. But her body was as lush and full as that of a much older woman; the tiny waist was beautifully emphasized by her rounded hips and high full bust. The look on her face—which bore a strong resemblance to Johnny's—was nothing short of radiance.

"Mama! Guess what?" Her brown eyes sparkled as she waved a long envelope.

"You got the scholarship!" With one movement mother and daughter were in each other's arms. "I just knew you would."

"I wasn't so sure—" She stopped at the sight of Rachel's smiling face. "You must be Johnny's new girl."

"Dolly!" said Deenie, laughing. "You talk like Johnny brings home a new one every other day." To Rachel she said, "That couldn't be further from the truth, really. Johnny always had girls chasing after him. They used to call or drive by or think up some reason to drop in. But he's picky as the dickens." She smiled at Rachel. "Though I'll have to admit he never brought anybody like you home. Dolly, this is Dr. Rachel McGeary."

"You're a doctor?" The girl's tone was awed. "Where did you go to school? Did it take a really long time? How did you get the money?"

Rachel held up her hands, laughing. "Wait, wait! One question at a time. Now first of all, I—"

"I'll leave you two to get acqainted," said Deenie, obviously pleased at the instant rapport between her daughter and this interesting young woman her son had brought home. She picked up the tray and left them to their conversation.

Chapter Six

After Jim Allen returned to work, Johnny said he was going to look up an old friend and leave Rachel with his mother and sister. When Rachel asked about the friend, they exchanged a look that made her really curious.

"Oh," said Deenie casually, "he and Johnny went to school together. Joe Bob's a couple of years younger, but he's been pretty wild. Not like Johnny—"

"But, Mama," broke in Dolly, "he's settled down a lot this last year."

"Maybe so, Dolly, but not enough for..." She smiled brightly and asked Rachel a question which turned the conversation in an entirely different direction.

Though Rachel was still curious about Johnny's friend, she was content to spend the afternoon getting acquainted with Johnny's mother and sister. She found the two a fascinating pair.

Deenie was laughing now as she watched Dolly set the table for supper. "You should have seen her as a youngster, always patching up some critter, whether it wanted patching or not! I made up my mind a long time ago she'd have her chance."

The girl flashed her mother a smile that touched Rachel deeply. Hesitantly she said, "I take it from, well, from several things I've picked up this afternoon that your husband feels Dolly should—"

Dolly set down a glass a little harder than she should have. "He thinks I ought to marry Tommy Votaw and have a bunch of babies."

"And that's not what you want?" Rachel asked.

"Oh, maybe. But first I want to go to college. I don't want to just stay here without at least seeing what's out there." She paused, then added slowly, her fine brown eyes serious. "I may not even be able to get through all the training."

Her mother's voice was low and intense as she said, "But you deserve a chance to find out!"

Rachel said thoughtfully, "Come for a walk with me, Dolly? I'd like to see the Thicket up close, but from what I hear you need a guide."

Deenie nodded. "That's no joke. It may not be like it used to be, but you can still get lost mighty easy."

"Coming with us, Deenie?"

"No, Rachel, you two go on. I'll just finish up here."

Outside the air was almost humid enough to bathe in, but alive and sweet with honeysuckle and magnolia and the heavy, musky odors of the encroaching woods. They hadn't gone far, when they came upon a little log house, its deep front porch dim and inviting.

"Oh, it's beautiful!" exclaimed Rachel.

Dolly's expression was a little surprised. "You really think so? Mama would be tickled. It's hers."

"Would she mind if we took a look inside?"

"No, she wouldn't mind." A mischievous grin lit her face. "Daddy calls it her playhouse."

They walked up onto the porch, their feet echoing on the age-roughed boards. There were a pair of old high-backed rockers, with the original cane seats, and between them was a homely but graceful stick table. A split oak basket with a lovely bunch of dried wildflowers in it was on the table, and on the walls behind was a fascinating assortment of antique tools.

Inside Dolly lit a pair of kerosene lamps. The soft glow showed a room that was surely a close approximation of the way a homemaker a hundred years ago might have arranged it. A fine trestle table was graced by a beautiful, smoothly carved dough bowl; the corner cupboard was full, but not cluttered, with blue and gray spongeware; the pie safe was a wonderful example of the tincrafter's art.

In the other corner of the room a rope-strung bed was covered with a Rose of Sharon quilt, and several other fine quilts were folded artfully on the wooden blanket rack beside the bed. Everywhere she looked there were deft little touches, small necessities of the home in the past century.

"It's almost like a museum," Rachel said in awe.

"That's close to the truth," said Dolly. "Except that's way far from what Mama sees."

Rachel went over to the worn drainboard to admire a fine collection of kitchen utensils in the split-cane tray. "What do you mean, Dolly?"

"All this," the girl waved a hand gracefully in the air, "is just a means to an end to Mama. Oh, I don't mean she doesn't enjoy collecting and trading and getting it all together here." That mischievous grin curved her mouth again. "Daddy's right, though. It is like a playhouse for Mama." Her face grew serious now. "But every week or two she goes into Beaumont with a load of stuff, and Mama's a real smart businesswoman."

"Businesswoman?" echoed Rachel, puzzled now.

"She sells things to antique dealers and never fails to make a profit," Dolly said proudly. "People around here, at least lots of them, want new stuff, modern things. A lot of these things they'd just throw out if Mama didn't pay them. But Daddy doesn't know—" She halted, looking as though she suddenly wondered if she should have kept quiet.

Rachel couldn't help but laugh a little. "What you're saying is that your mother has a thriving business here, and your daddy thinks she's just playing house."

"If he ever asked, she'd tell him. But Mama wants me

to go to college, and...and I want to!" Dolly's chin lifted. "She's got enough saved for me to go the first two years, anyway."

"I see." And Rachel did, now. Deenie Allen was just quietly making sure that her daughter got the chance she deserved. Thoughtfully she said, "Dolly, your folks seem to get along really well."

"They do. Mama thinks Daddy hung the moon, and he never has looked at another woman since he laid eyes on her. I hope I get a man someday who'll love me like he does her," she added shyly.

"Me, too," murmured Rachel, about to say something more when she heard Johnny call.

"Doc, you in there?"

He came through the door, ducking his head under the split log frame, and for a moment Rachel's heart almost hurt at the sight of his marvelously active face, his lean, strong body. *I'd better watch myself*, she thought. Never before in her life had she been so intensely physically attracted to a man. "Hi," she said softly, thinking he looked as though he were ready to kiss her.

He didn't, though he did slip an arm around her shoulders as another young man came in. "Someone I want you to meet. This is my old buddy, Joe Bob Connor."

The blond young man shyly put out his work hardened hand. "Pleased to meet you, Miss, uh, Doctor."

"Just Rachel is fine." She shook his hand, liking the way he met her eyes.

A smile transformed his homely face. "Me and Johnny thought maybe you'd like to go to the rodeo over at Livingston."

"How about me?" asked Dolly.

Joe Bob smiled admiringly at the lissome Dolly. "Well, I'd sure like to take you, but your daddy told me I was too old for you last time I asked."

With a toss of her dark, heavy hair, Dolly said, "Oh, I'm old enough to decide for myself who I want to go out with. I'm eighteen now!"

Joe Bob let his eyes dwell on the girl's lush figure for only a moment. She was, after all, his friend's sister. "We'd better ask him all the same," he said regretfully, as though he knew it was hopeless.

Jim Allen said no, as they'd expected, then slyly suggested that they attend the revival services at the church instead. Joe Bob looked pained for a moment, stole a glance at Dolly, and said, "Sure, why not," all the while trying to ignore Jim's glowering look. It was obvious Jim hadn't expected him to accept.

As they changed clothes in the girl's frilly bedroom, Dolly's excitement spilled over, infecting Rachel. "I just can't believe you've never been to a rodeo! Wish we were going to one tonight, instead of to church. Why, Johnny says they have ropings every week at the FFA arena in Marvin and several rodeos all year. The Fourth of July, Memorial Day, Labor Day—" She stopped, then said, "Say, Monday is Labor Day, isn't it?"

Rachel nodded. "And pretty soon, it'll be fall."

"It's awful nice here in the Thicket then, when the sweet gum trees turn neat colors and—"

"You two about ready?" Johnny called as he knocked at the door.

When Rachel opened the door and Johnny saw her in the white skirt and blouse with delicate crochet trim, he just stood there for a moment. Then he softly said, "You are something else."

"What?" she asked teasingly.

Before he could answer, Dolly came up beside Rachel. "Save it, big brother, and get me out of the house before Daddy changes his mind. I'd rather go to the rodeo, but I'll do anything—even go to church on Saturday night—to get out of the house."

"All right, Sis," he said, his eyes still on Rachel. He leaned close to her and whispered, "I'll tell you later."

"Turn right where the coyote skins hang on the

fence, go a mile and a half...." Rachel couldn't keep the laughter from her voice. "That's actually the way you give directions to the church?"

"That's right," said Dolly from the back seat of Rachel's car. "It's a real old church, but pretty."

"Yeah, pretty," muttered Joe Bob.

Johnny glanced back at his friend, knowing that even if he went to church from now on his attraction to Dolly was hopeless. Jim Allen would die before he let Dolly marry a man like Joe Bob...even if he had calmed down. "I came to know the Lord in that church. There were a bunch of us that came forward during revival services just like they're holding this week. They baptized us in Sandy Creek."

Dolly gave an elaborate shudder. "I can't stand to think about it! What if there had been a big old water moccasin...?"

"Well," said Johnny, his hand finding Rachel's, "there wasn't."

"I'd like to have been there," she said, wishing they were alone and not feeling the least bit guilty about it.

"If I remember right," said Joe Bob, "the preacher was that old bird, what was his name?"

"J.B. McKinny," supplied Johnny.

"Right. I even came to hear him a few times. He told good fox hunting stories."

"Joe Bob, is that all you came for?" asked Dolly pertly.

"Well, that and to see the girls," Joe Bob admitted.

"You're awful!" scolded Dolly, but she was smiling. "Oh, look, Rachel, there's the church. Don't you think it's pretty?"

Rachel had to admit it was, indeed, pretty. A plain rectangular structure covered with narrow white clapboards, it looked as though it had been freshly painted, right up to the cupola which held a bell. Each of the windows along either side had been carefully cut in a modest Gothic arch, and the opaque glass in them was wavy-looking and golden. Light flowed from them, making bright shapes on the ground. As the group got out of the car they could hear the bell's peal mingling sweetly with the sound of a choir practicing.

Rachel took a deep breath and summoned a smile. It was never easy for her to face a group of strangers, particularly since this group would be intensely interested in seeing who was with Johnny Allen. However, she'd overcome her natural shyness fairly well during her years of rigorous schooling, and the training stood her in good stead now as the onslaught began.

There were probably only thirty-five or forty people present, but not many, if any at all, missed meeting Rachel. They didn't miss the chance to comment on Joe Bob Connor's unprecedented appearance with Dolly, either. Joe Bob squirmed at their curious glances, especially when Deenie and Jim Allen came in, Jim's keen eyes on them.

When they finally settled down—brought to the long oak pews by the slow, wavy call of a Hammond organ set with full tremolo—Rachel felt the expectancy, the excitement hovering in the sultry air.

The first congregational song dragged so terribly it was painful for Rachel, who liked her hymns on the peppy side. It evidently pained the valiantly struggling song leader, too. He grasped the sides of the sturdy wooden pulpit and said hopefully, "Say, as y'all've probably noticed, our piano player is kinda noticeable by her absence." A little spattering of laughter encouraged him to go on. "Mrs. Jansen over here on the organ is doing a fine job, but she sure could use some backup. Anybody out there care to help us out on the piano this evening?" His earnest young face searched the crowd hopefully, and brightened when Johnny pointed to Rachel, nodding.

"Johnny!" she whispered. But he was already gently nudging her up, and there wasn't much she could do but walk to the piano and sit down. An apologetic little smile played on her lips as she looked into the skeptical face of the organist.

"Thank you, Miss McGeary," he said brightly. "Would you play an introduction for number 335? Now, on your feet, people, we can't sing 'Standing on the Promises' and sit on the premises." They all dutifully got to their feet, and almost all of them curiously, expectantly watched Rachel.

Rachel was by no means a brilliant accompanist, but she was adequate, and she had excellent rhythm. She was gratified by the almost comical look of relief on the young songleader's face as she launched spiritedly into the introduction. She'd been told once that if you intend to kill a song, it's better to run it to death than drag it to death. The organist's glowering face hinted she was of the opposite persuasion! But the young man waving his hands enthusiastically agreed with Rachel—they sang five more songs. Rachel loved every minute of it.

When the evangelist rose to speak, his tie was already loosened, and it ended up on the back of his chair, along with his jacket, halfway through a rather fiery sermon. The murmured "amens" seemed to spur him on. Five people responded to his invitation, but Joe Bob Connor wasn't one of them, though his face was serious, even troubled during the extended invitation.

After they all sang "To God Be the Glory," the song leader said, "Folks let's all give our little pianist (he accented the *a*, instead of the *i*) a big hand!" When they did, wholeheartedly, the young man added, "That's good, that's good. You people know I believe in giving flares to the living."

Rachel smiled and nodded. It took her a couple of seconds to realize he was saying, "flowers to the living."

Deenie, Jim, Johnny, and Dolly all gathered around Rachel, delighted that she fit in so well and could play the piano to boot.

Jim nodded. "We appreciate your helping out." He turned to Dolly. "Dolly, girl, maybe you'd best come on home with your mama and me."

"Oh, Daddy, don't make me!" pleaded Dolly.

"Now, girl, you'll do as I say," he said, his eyes narrowed.

"She'll be fine with us, Mr. Allen," said Rachel, aware too late that her tone was awfully firm. She tried to soften it by adding, "Johnny and I will watch out for her—really we will."

"She should come home with us, like I said," Jim Allen repeated stubbornly.

"Now Jim, Dolly is—" began Deenie, but just then Joe Bob cut in, his voice hard.

"I've got to meet some of the fellas, so I'll see you later, Johnny." As he turned to go, he cast one look at Dolly, one at her father. Then he left without another word.

Rachel thought the looks were eloquent. Joe Bob Connor was painfully aware that not only was he not good enough to take Jim Allen's daughter out, he wasn't even good enough to come to church with her. A frown creasing her brow, Rachel said, "That's really too bad—that he left, I mean. I think Joe Bob was close to making a decision tonight."

"And I suppose you think it was my fault he didn't?"

A little taken back at Jim Allen's sudden intense question, she replied, "I didn't say that at all, Mr. Allen."

"A man's got a right to protect his own flesh and blood," he said, "especially his daughter."

The others in the group were silent. None of them looked at Jim or Rachel, who said quietly, "Of course you do, when she needs protection."

He stared hard at Rachel for a moment, but said nothing more to her. Instead he turned to his wife and daughter. "You two come on. It's time we headed on home."

Deenie's look was regretful as it rested briefly on Rachel; Dolly's face was closed and sullen. But both women followed Jim Allen's ramrod-straight back from the little church.

Stricken, Rachel said, "Oh, Johnny, I'm sorry. I shouldn't have interfered. I don't know what got into me, except that he's so...so—"

"Yes, he is." Johnny's hand on her elbow was warm as he guided her out and into the car.

When they reached the Allen house, Rachel wasn't sure what to expect. It certainly wasn't the elaborately polite front Jim put up. It was as though the incident hadn't happened, except that Dolly obviously was holed up in her room and Deenie's eyes showed the strain. She kept trying to offer them cake, a piece of chicken left over from supper—something. Rachel, who couldn't have eaten a bite, kept thinking of nice ways of refuse.

"I've eaten so much already I could roll back to Marvin, without the car," she said ruefully.

For the first time since they'd come into the house, Jim's reply seemed natural. "Why, girl, it'd take an awful lot to spoil that figure of yours. Besides," he said as he pulled the plump Deenie close, "I like a woman with some meat on her bones."

"Well, a walk wouldn't hurt," replied Rachel, grateful to see Jim's mood lighten. "But I don't know if Johnny's up to it."

"If he's not up to a walk in the moonlight with a pretty woman, he's in bad shape," said Jim his eyes showing a faint glimmer of what Rachel interpreted as the desire to let things proceed as normally as possible.

Not under any illusions that he'd forgotten her interference, Rachel nonetheless accepted the gesture for what it was. "How about it, Johnny?"

"We don't have to walk far," he said easily, placing an arm around her shoulders.

"I think he's got something besides exercise on his mind, Rachel," teased Jim. "Watch him."

Deenie tousled his thick russet hair. "Maybe you'd

better not go after all, Rachel."

"She's one to give advice." Jim squeezed her closer. "We took lots of moonlight walks, too, and look where it got us."

Johnny whispered into Rachel's ear. "Come on, let's slip out. They probably won't even notice we're gone."

Rachel nodded; Deenie and Jim were certainly immersed in one another. She made a remark to that effect as they strolled down the path to the little log house, carefully adjusting her stride to accommodate his stiff-legged one.

"Let's sit here on Mama's playhouse porch and listen to the bull frogs," he suggested, pulling her down beside him as he sat on the edge of the porch.

"Your parents are fun to watch," said Rachel, having decided to avoid the unpleasant topic of Dolly and Joe Bob. "They're more like kids in love than parents."

"They've always been like that. And after all these years they still look at each other moony-eyed."

"I think it's wonderful," said Rachel softly. "You never really said much about them."

He pulled his good knee up and clasped it in both hands. "I wondered what you'd think. Growing up like you did, with only Miz Mac, it must have been difficult for you to get a picture of the way a family ought to be."

"Johnny," she said suddenly and against her better judgment, "do you think it's right for your mother to wait on your dad the way she does?"

He glanced over at her in the darkness, as though he'd like to see the expression on her face. "Why? I never thought much about it."

"Think about it now."

He was silent for a few moments. Then he said, "Mama does exactly what she wants, Rachel."

"You're sure of that, are you?"

"Why, I just never thought much about it," he repeated.

Rachel started to press the point and ask him what he

thought of his mother's business venture in the little house behind them. But she decided it was very possible he didn't know about it any more than Jim did. She also decided she'd probably done enough poking her nose where she had no business for one day. His hand was caressing the back of her neck gently.

"Rachel, I...." He pulled her slowly to him, and leaned close to kiss her mouth, a light tender kiss that made her shiver and pull back, intensely aware of the effect he had on her.

He didn't kiss her again, but neither did he take his hand from her neck. A sound very much like a chuckle escaped his lips. "It's been a long time since I sat on a porch in the moonlight with a girl. I'm out of practice."

Rachel took a deep breath to stabilize her and her feelings. "Oh, you don't seem out of practice to me. What I'd like to know is—" She hesitated, unwilling to ask the question that had been lurking in the back of her mind almost since she'd met him.

"What were you about to say?"

He sounded as though he wanted very much to know. His fingers had wandered from her neck to her shoulder and traced shivering patterns on her bare skin. She caught his hand, holding it tightly. "Well, how you've escaped all these years?"

"You mean marriage?"

"Um hm." Rachel wondered why she felt so anxious. After all, it was just an objective discussion.

"I was waiting for you."

For a moment her heart seemed to stop beating. He sounded so gently, terribly serious. Vaguely aware of how silly her next words seemed, she said, "Oh, Johnny, be serious."

"You think I'm not?" He held her hand to his chest, and she felt the steady beat of his heart through the thin cotton fabric of his shirt. "Rachel, I'm sort of..." He hesitated, then said, "Well, maybe hot-blooded is the only way you could say it and be truthful. And since I was sixteen there have been girls willing to give me what any young man is supposedly on the prowl for. But..."

He trailed off again, and Rachel waited, hardly noticing that she held her breath. She didn't say anything, but she felt the flow of energy through his hand, his body. "It was in that same little church we went to tonight that God spoke to my heart. I listened and answered yes to Him. After that, the more I thought about it—and read the book of Proverbs—the more I decided casual sex just wasn't for me. You know what I mean?"

"Yes, I do."

"Anyway, I decided early on that I wanted it all—friendship, sex, and love. It seems to me that God wants only the best for us." His smile was barely visible in the darkness. "And as you've noticed, I want the best."

The calm, absolute assurance in his voice awed and excited Rachel at the same time. "I've never heard a man talk about these things like you do. It's...I like it."

"That's good," he murmured. The frog chorus that had swelled to a croaking crescendo stopped suddenly, as though it had been orchestrated. Both Rachel and Johnny sat quietly in the sudden, lovely stillness. Then, here and there on either side of the house, a few of the huge croakers began to tune in until there was a full chorus again. "How about you?"

"What do you mean?"

"Oh, if you were a Thicket girl and unmarried at your age, you'd have to be cross-eyed or bowlegged, or otherwise unmarriageable. You're certainly not that."

She laughed a little. "Don't be too sure. I used to wonder. In high school I was painfully shy and not too pretty, either—"

"I have a hard time believing that."

She went on as though he hadn't spoken. "Maybe the worst thing was that I loved school."

"You're kidding!"

"No, I'm not. I loved to study and made a 4.0 grade

average almost every semester. The only time I didn't was once when I was sick and failed P.E. It brought my GPA down to a 3.98."

"Pity," he murmured unsympathetically.

"It was," she flared back. "I had my heart set on a perfect 4.0. I never got asked out much. High school boys don't like girls they think are smarter than they are. It was awful."

"How about after you got to college?"

"Not much better. They asked me out, but I always ended up fighting my way out of the car. I stopped dating almost entirely. And when I got to medical school I was totally involved in *becoming a doctor*, and...." She hesitated, then went on. "The right man just never came along."

"And nothing less than right will do, will it?"

"No," she whispered, so faintly he bent closer to hear.

"Rachel, you feel it too, don't you?"

"What?" The word was only a breath against his ear.

"This is something special between us. It started in your emergency room, and it keeps getting stronger."

"But is feeling enough...?"

He stopped her words with a kiss and she leaned nearer, the ache to be even nearer filling her body. When he pulled away he murmured, "Believe me when I tell you I have never, in all my life, had this particular set of feelings for any woman, Rachel. Believe me."

She put her arms around his neck, tight, and whispered, "I believe you." Then, she lost herself in the warmth of his closeness, the strength of his body.

Chapter Seven

Rachel had begun to wonder how she would make it through the week without seeing Johnny. He must have wondered the same thing because he showed up just before dinnertime on Thursday evening. Though he protested—weakly—Miz Mac insisted on setting another place at the table for him, telling him that Stan Janek was staying and there was plenty of gumbo.

At this pronouncement, Johnny grinned and pulled up a chair. "Over near Honey Island there's a Cajun lady who makes a mighty fine living making gumbo. I can hear her now...'First you make a—'"

"Roux!" Rachel finished for him.

"Can you make gumbo?" he asked, looking at Rachel in her lemon-yellow shirtwaist dress. It made her look like a ray of pure sunlight.

Her color was high. If he'd commented on it she'd have said it was from the heat of the kitchen, which wasn't altogether true. It was mostly due to the pleasant surprise of finding him at the door, thought Rachel, as she placed the tureen in the center of the table. All she said aloud was, "Sure, I can make gumbo. But Stan brought this. Smells good, doesn't it?"

Stan, his face genial with a whimsical smile, said, "Buncie, my cook, could work wherever she wanted to. I'll have to admit I pay her plenty to stay with me.

Some of those River Oaks ladies are forever trying to lure her away, but she's been with me almost thirty years now."

Miz Mac smiled at him. "Stan, any dinner guest who brings dinner is welcome. You're a smart man." She had on a deep blue caftan and turban to match tonight. Although she was pale, her blue eyes sparkled and picked up the color she wore.

"Evidently not smart enough to catch the most interesting woman I ever met."

"Now Stan," Miz Mac said, "if I've told you once I've told you a hundred times, you're thirty years too late!"

"You look younger than springtime to me," Stan murmured.

"Whew," breathed Johnny. When Rachel frowned at him he winked back at her.

Hoping the sudden rush of warmth she felt didn't show on her face, she said, "Johnny, will you please get the rolls? They're on the kitchen table."

"Sure." He rose lazily, his eyes bright with mischief and holding hers. "No telling what ideas I might get in this steamy atmosphere."

Rachel started to tell him to act his age, but stopped at the realization that Stan Janek was well over twice Johnny's age. Relieved when Johnny went into the other room, she took the moment to check and make sure everything was in order.

The long, gracefully proportioned room had a row of tall casement windows along one side and a large bay window overlooking the back yard. Miz Mac had filled it with flowering plants from the shop. They made a vivid, stimulating focus for the plain oak sideboard and long dining table. Rachel found matches in the carved box on the mantel over the lovely fireplace and had lit all but the last of the tall white tapers when Johnny came into the room with a silver basket of rolls in his hand.

Miz Mac and Stan happened to look up just then and

see Johnny's face as he watched Rachel light the last candle. Her face was illuminated in the soft glow, and the golden shimmers in her hair, caught at the nape of her neck with a ribbon, seemed to take Johnny's breath away.

"Now who's moonstruck?" asked Stan slyly.

Johnny started to say something, but the phone rang. "I'll get it, and if it's for the Doc I'll tell 'em she's busy," he said instead.

Rachel laughed. "Tempting, but don't you dare." She watched as Johnny spoke jauntily into the receiver, pretending to be a butler. When his face grew still and grave and he handed it to her with a murmured apology, she felt that little tightening of her stomach she always did at the possibility of a life-threatening situation. "Yes, this is Dr. McGeary. Slow down, Mrs. Blanton, and start again." She paused, then said, "I see. Any temperature? Well, take it, and don't give her anything more by mouth. I'll be right over." After another word or two of reassurance, she hung up. "Sorry about the dinner party, Aunt Lyddy, but these two fine gentlemen can keep you company."

She was already moving from the room when Johnny spoke. "I'm going with you." He turned to Stan. "Mr. Janek, you can hold the fort here, can't you?"

"My boy, there's nothing I'd like better. I brought a couple of videocassettes—Charlie Chaplin and the Keystone Cops."

"Oh, really, I'd like to see those." His eyes were on the door. Rachel had disappeared.

"It's a shame you'll miss them, but you'd better go on and take care of that pretty little doctor." Even as he spoke to Johnny, Stan was smiling at Miz Mac.

"Yes," she said, "you go on, Johnny. We'll be fine. Only I've got a notion that 'pretty little doctor' is tougher in the long haul than either of you. I raised her, didn't I?" Her face showed her pride in her niece. "Stan, you serve. The rice first, and then the gumbo.

81

And I like my salad with it, not before it."

Johnny found Rachel already outside, tossing her black bag into the back seat of her car. "Hey, weren't you going to wait for me?"

"If you got here in time, yes," she said. Not coolly, not teasingly, just matter of factly. "Get in. They live a good ways out South Winfree."

Johnny barely got his door shut before the little car roared into action. Rachel expertly slipped it into gear and zoomed off into the darkness.

The Blanton home was a modest one. They were met by a worried-faced woman, her skin made sallow by the yellow bug bulb that hung naked from a cord on the porch ceiling.

"Oh, Dr. McGeary, I'm so glad to see you! Dr. Burleigh's answering machine kept saying he was temporarily unavailable, and we don't know any other doctors. My husband knew your daddy—"

Rachel didn't waste any emotion at the news that she'd called Burleigh first. "Where is Jenny, Mrs. Blanton? And what happened?"

The woman led the way down the narrow hall, looking back as she spoke. "She fell off her bicycle. I guess the handlebar turned and poked her real hard right under her ribs."

"Which side?"

"What?" The woman looked blank for a second, then said, "Oh, the left. There's hardly even a bruise, though, and I thought she'd be all right, but she threw up all her supper, and she keeps moaning about how much it hurts. She even asked me to call a doctor, and she sure has never done that!"

The room they entered was small, and the air was very close with the odor of sickness. But the bed on which the child was huddled was neatly made with clean sheets, and as Rachel laid a hand on her forehead, Jenny Blanton's brown eyes flew open, a startled question in them. Rachel sat beside her and spoke in a calm, soothing tone. "I'm Dr. McGeary, Jenny, and I've come to make you feel better." Even as she spoke her hand was smoothing back the damp light brown hair. The child relaxed visibly, only tensing a little as Rachel asked, "Is it all right if I check your tummy?"

Jenny nodded, eyes wide as Rachel pulled back the sheet and gently palpated the little girl's abdomen. *Hard and rigid*, she thought. There was swift, sharp intake of breath from the child as she pressed on the upper left quadrant. "Sorry, honey," she murmured. As Rachel took the child's blood pressure, her mind was simultaneously noting other symptoms: Jenny's pressure was very low, and she was diaphoretic...cool and clammy, and very pale.

Rachel rose and went to the doorway where the child's mother and Johnny stood. "Of course I can't be absolutely certain, but I think she's bleeding internally. We need to do an exploratory laparotomy. I'm afraid she may have ruptured her spleen in that fall."

Mrs. Blanton couldn't stifle the gasp that came to her lips. "Oh! that sounds awful!"

"If that's what is causing the problem, I'm almost certain we can fix it. Your husband, is he here?"

"He's out of town on a job." The helplessness, the indecision she felt showed in the tightness around her mouth, her hunched shoulders.

"Mrs. Blanton, if you want my advice—"

The woman interrupted Rachel. "I do...please."

"We should get Jenny to the hospital right away. Johnny—Mr. Allen and I—will take you both, if you like."

"I'll sit in the back seat and hold her," volunteered Johnny.

"I—" Once again the woman's face showed the agony of having to make decisions alone. Then, she exhaled, the long gusty sigh filling the little hallway. "All right. I'd never forgive myself if anything happened to her. Her daddy's always bragging about what a fine little 'girl she is. We didn't have but one. No boys, but—"

Rachel stopped the nervous flood of words with a hand on the woman's arm. "Do you have a blanket we can wrap her in?"

"I'll carry her," said Johnny, stepping into the room.

"Your leg—" protested Rachel, but he held up a hand and she knew he'd carry Jenny or die trying. "I'll start the car. Thanks for being here, Johnny," she added softly.

The ride to the hospital was a short one, but Rachel's mind was busily working. Jenny would need blood. She'd know how much after the hematocrit. She'd have to check the donor list and call Seth Morely, the anesthesiologist. A smile curved her mouth. Seth was one of the best.

Nurse Patt. A scrub nurse of the old school, who could do everything from sterilizing her own instruments to acting as her own circulating nurse and never break the sterile field. *Yes*, thought Rachel with satisfaction, *the three of us can do it*.

Nurse Patt was not on duty, but she answered Rachel's call to her home immediately. Seth took a little longer, but by the time Rachel had cross matched Jenny's blood type and made certain the supply of packed cells was adequate, he was on his way. Johnny stood by quietly, watching Rachel as she got her small team together and remembered to reassure Jenny and her mother from time to time.

"There's no need for you to wait here," Rachel said to Johnny as soon as she had a free moment. "Why don't you go on over to Aunt Lyddy's? I'm sure there's still gumbo."

"I've been thinking."

"In the middle of all this?" Rachel's laughter was slightly breathless. They were in the hallway outside the emergency room, where Nurse Patt and the nurse on duty were preparing little Jenny Blanton for surgery. "Well, what about?"

"I'd like to watch you operate, if it's all right."

Rachel stared at him, searching for signs that he was joking, but his face was completely serious. "You do? Why?"

"Because..." He trailed off, then noticed her impatience. Knowing she hadn't much time, he added quickly, "Because it's you, an important part of you, and I want to know all about you."

"Sure you won't faint?"

He shook his head and moved with her as she walked toward the small operating room.

His mouth turned up a little. "Real men don't faint."

"I sure hope not, because if you do, we'll just have to let you lie where you fall."

"Don't worry, I—" He was interrupted as a tall, very thin man burst through the back doors.

"Seth!" said Rachel, obviously pleased to see him. "I'm just going in to scrub." Seth was not a handsome man by any standards. He had the long face of a melancholy afghan hound, and his long legs were encased in Levi's and looked like a stork's. But there was a keen intelligence in his eyes, and his complete attention to Rachel's terse words about Jenny's case precluded any introductions. It wasn't until Johnny murmured a question that Rachel looked up, almost as though she was surprised to see him there, and introduced him briefly to Seth.

Johnny didn't speak to either of them after that, just closely followed their example as they scrubbed their hands, wrists, and arms until he thought they might all be down to the second layer of skin. With an effort he kept himself from chuckling at the sight of the lanky Seth in greens, his cowboy boots stuffed into the shapeless bootees worn to prevent sparks in the operating room where volatile fluids and oxygen were going to be in use.

Seth grinned as he saw Johnny staring at his boots. "I always did say I'd die with my boots on," he drawled, "so I guess it's okay to work in 'em."

Before Johnny could reply Rachel came into the operating room, and he was struck by how different she looked. The loose, impersonal hospital greens, especially the cap she wore over her hair, made her almost sexless. Almost...he thought with a small inner smile. Only her eyes showed above the mask and he was struck by how extraordinarily beautiful they were, how expressive. He was sure no man ever had eyes like that.

Johnny stayed well out of the way as the little team launched into action. The brilliant lights above the operating table lent the scene an aura of dramatic unreality, but when Seth murmured to Jenny, sedated now, that she must breathe deeply and count backwards, Johnny was all too aware that this was real.

Rachel's voice was clear and low. "She under yet, Seth?" When he answered affirmitively she asked, "What are her vitals?"

"The first unit is hanging, so her BP is 90 over 64, pulse is 112. Fairly stable."

Nurse Patt stood silently, ready with an awesome array of instruments. And then Rachel began. With an assurance that awed Johnny, she boldly made a transverse incision into the child's upper abdomen. Quickly she and Nurse Patt tied off the bleeders, and it seemed only seconds before Rachel had found the lacerated organ and lifted it carefully to the fore of the incision.

He was a little startled in the stillness, to hear Rachel say, "Even though we're only repairing it, we'll have to mobilize the spleen just as though we were going to perform a splenectomy, or remove it entirely." Johnny realized she was speaking for his benefit. He swallowed hard at the sight of the large rip in the small, sort of pear-shaped mass that was the little girl's spleen.

As Rachel gently picked off the clotted material she also cauterized several bleeding points. The smell was not pleasant. "I'm trying to make certain all the splenic tissue we leave is viable. You know, or maybe you don't, that for a long time the removal of ruptured spleens was considered a low-risk procedure."

"But no more," muttered Seth, "no more."

"Why not?" Johnny felt obligated to ask, and hated the breathy sound of his words.

"Oh," answered Rachel, her small gloved hands still working surely, "first of all, there was a remarkable increase of complications, even deaths, in the early post-op period following removal of the spleen. Besides that, there is now firm evidence that when you lose your spleen, nothing in the body takes over its function."

"Which means your immune system doesn't work so good." Nurse Patt handed Rachel a sponge. "And that's really important, especially in children."

"So you always leave them in, now?" Johnny felt a little woozy, especially every time he heard the whirring hiss of the cautery needle. He told himself that he'd die on his feet and stiffen upright before he'd faint and fall. It certainly didn't help that every time Rachel used the cautery needle, the heart monitor showed a straight line for a second or two. The word for that, he thought, is discombobulating.

"When it's possible." Rachel's clear gray eyes met his for a moment. Her dark lashes didn't blink. "But some doctors are still skeptical and remove the damaged spleen as a matter of course, just as they always did."

"What are Jenny's chances?" Johnny asked.

"Good." Rachel carefully finished suturing the tear, placed a yellowish white material on the wound, then tucked the spleen back into its place near the diaphragm and in front of the kidneys. "Let's close, Nurse Patt. Seth, her vitals?"

"BP 108 over 72. Pulse, 72. She's stable."

Rachel nodded, and began to close the incision. Johnny was again awed by the dexterity, the sureness of her swift, slender fingers. She didn't speak much now;

there was no need. Seth could be trusted to monitor the child's vital signs, and Nurse Patt anticipated Rachel's every need without her asking.

It wasn't long before Johnny could see the procedure was at an end. He slipped out, pulling off the cap and mask as he went outside, grateful to be able to breathe the night air. As fascinating as it had been, he felt weak, as though he might pass out after all.

He looked up at the star-filled sky and took a half dozen great gulping breaths of air—fresh air, free from the intimidating odors of the operating room. The short time he'd held her slight body in the car had made him feel quite close to little Jenny, even responsible for her in a strange way, and he was grateful she was going to be all right. But his overriding emotion was awe—awe that a tiny woman like Rachel could make such a difference in a life. It boggled his mind and gave him an entirely new perspective on her.

Knowing it would be a while before Rachel could leave her young patient, Johnny settled his back against the side of the building, content for the moment to be out of the operating room and in the open air. He was all too aware that he had been as out of his element in there as he'd ever been in his entire life. But Rachel had been totally at home, at ease and very much in charge of herself and the situation.

It was just before dawn when Rachel came out, satisfied that Jenny was stabilized. She and Johnny walked out into the still, pre-dawn air. She laughed, then clapped a hand over her mouth as she almost stumbled with fatigue. "You're supposed to be the one who has trouble walking! Oh, I'm so tired I can't see straight. If I remember right, my day started at this time yesterday. Whew! This has almost been like my intern days."

"You'll have to tell me all about them," said Johnny, his arm around her shoulders as they made their way to the car.

"How about after breakfast? I missed lunch yesterday,

and you know what happened to dinner." She sighed. "I wonder if shrimp gumbo is good for breakfast."

"Yaurghhh." Johnny's gutteral eloquence showed exactly what he thought of that idea. "I'll make you some of my special scrambled eggs." He handed her in, then went around and climbed in himself.

"What makes them so special?" Rachel's words were mumbles as she tried to curl up on the seat of the car.

"You'll see," he said with a trace of smugness.

Half an hour later at Miz Mac's Rachel had to admit his scrambled eggs were every bit as unusual as he'd claimed. Good, she'd told him, but...different. He took that as a compliment as he ate the last of his. He'd put in minced green onion, green peppers, mushrooms and cheese. Then after carefully scrambling them, he put a dollop of warmed salsa on top.

"Sure, it looks disgusting," he admitted cheerfully, "but it tastes good."

"How did you discover this...great recipe?" She allowed herself to stare dreamily at him across the polished oak table. Even at a quarter of six in the morning his eyes seemed to have that marvelous mischievous look. She wanted to touch him, to see what the faint shadow on his jaw felt like.

"I could tell you it's an old family recipe—"

"But it's not, is it?" she responded to his merry challenge.

"Nope. I just kept trying to make Spanish omelets and kept getting Mexican scrambled." He stood up and stretched mightily.

Rachel couldn't believe her reaction to the sight of him stretching his arms and flexing his shoulders. *Get hold of yourself, Doc. He's just a man.* And some other part of herself whispered back, *Oh no, he's not. He's ...more.*

"Let's go out and watch the sun come up," he said softly.

"You've got to work today," she protested, but faintly. "And so do I."

"And we'll both work better if we can think back every once in a while and remember how we watched the sunrise...together. Come on." He pulled her toward the French doors in the back. Rachel didn't protest any further because she didn't want to.

Outside they were greeted by the sleepy sound of a mockingbird which had probably been singing for hours. Rachel stood quietly, taking deep breaths of the cool, fragrant air. Johnny came up behind her and wrapped his arms around her waist, drawing her very close to his body.

The closeness gave her the courage to voice a thought that had just surfaced. "Johnny," she began, then stopped as he nuzzled the back of her neck.

"Know what Mama used to tell us kids when we were little?" Rachel could only shake her head. "That this hollow right here at the back of your neck—" He softly kissed her neck just below the hairline and she shivered. "—is your sweet place. She'd grab us and and kiss us there, and we yelled and screamed and—"

"And secretly loved every minute of it." She turned in his arms and looked up at him. "Johnny, I'm really sorry I upset your father. Sometimes I'm kind of blunt and say things I shouldn't."

He shrugged. "Forget it."

She saw the slight withdrawal in his eyes. "He won't, will he?"

For a long while he stared off into the pecan trees, watching the faint light chase away the shadows there. Then he said, "No, probably not. Daddy has some mighty definite ideas about the way things ought to be."

And I didn't fit many of them, Rachel thought. Aloud she asked, "But didn't you ever...cross him?"

"Sure I did. But he expected that. He didn't like it, you understand, but he expected his son to challenge him."

The way he said *son* obviously meant that daughters

were in a whole different category. "But you have to admit he doesn't treat Dolly—or your mother—fairly."

"I don't have to admit anything," Johnny said, suddenly pulling her almost roughly to him, "except how impressed I was with you last night. You saved that little girl's life."

"Probably," admitted Rachel, reluctant to let the discussion about the weekend at his parents' home end there, but sensing it was going to be that way, at least for now.

"But as impressed as I was with you as a doctor, honey, it's nothing compared to the way I feel about you as a woman...." His hands moved on her back, massaging the tired muscles. She relaxed a little, giving in to the wonderful relief as his hands moved slowly, carefully to each shoulder, to the spot between that felt at times as though someone had hit her with a two-by-four, to the long muscles leading to her waist. Somewhere along the way the movements of his fingers stopped being therapeutic and became very, very sensual.

Rachel heard a little moan and knew that it was her own. "Johnny...," she breathed, but his lips stopped any more words. She gave herself to the kiss. Her arms were wound tightly around his body. She felt the taut muscles in his back and longed to caress them as he had hers, but without....She pulled back, inhaling once, exhaling all the way.

"I know." His voice was a little hoarse. "You've got to go in and get some sleep, and I've got a conference this morning." He made no move to go, however, for a long moment. Then he kissed the tip of her nose. "You've got the cutest nose in the world. Did you know that?"

He quickly walked away, leaving her standing there, listening to the sound of his car revving to life, out the driveway, and down the deserted street. Then, silence. Several more moments passed before she could make herself move and walk back into the house.

Chapter Eight

Finished with all her office appointments for the day, Rachel sat at her desk, pondering Lana Beth Duvall's file. She also carefully checked the notes she'd made at St. Joseph's library. The more she compared them, the more she was sure she had the answer: systemic lupus erythematosus, a disease in which the immune system malfunctions, a disease often misdiagnosed because it shows such widely different symptoms.

It wasn't too surprising that no one had suspected lupus before now. Besides herself and Burleigh, Lana Beth's husband had insisted on taking her to specialists, each of whom carefully concentrated on his own particular specialty. Rachel tapped a fingernail thoughtfully on Lana Beth's file and made a decision. After checking with Lana Beth, she'd make an appointment to see the kidney specialist and suggest that they begin the lab tests right away.

After making the calls, she gave in to another feeling that had been dogging her tracks, a general feeling of unease about Aunt Lyddy. She'd had it in varying degrees all week, and every evening when Johnny called they'd discussed it. He didn't agree that Miz Mac should stay home from the shop. He sided with her aunt, feeling that if she wanted to, she should be working.

She sighed. Their weeks had taken on a pattern imposed by both their busy schedules. Rachel, as the newest doctor in town, was on call for two weekends, off one. Johnny sometimes came in the middle of the week, but more often than not he just called every night. When Rachel had protested that his phone bill must be approaching the national debt, he'd laughed and said it was cheaper—if not as satisfactory—than a date.

So with Johnny's support Lyddy McGeary went to work as she always had. Her business was thriving, but she was looking even paler than before. Rachel gave in to her unease and decided to run over to the shop and check on her aunt, even though she'd emphatically been told not to.

Nonie met her at the door. "Oh, Rachel, honey, I'm *so* glad to see you! I tried to get her to take the afternoon off, but you know how she is, stubborn as a mule."

"What's wrong?" A sudden stab of fear ripped at Rachel.

"Oh, nothing horrible, just—"

"Nothing at all!" came Miz Mac's retort from the back room, where all the floral arrangements were made and the fine antique pieces were stripped and refinished.

Rachel followed Nonie back, and the look on her aunt's face showed she was in for trouble. "Aunt Lyddy," she began, determined to take the offensive, "I told you you've been doing too much! You're so pale and—"

"I'll have you know it's called a magnolia complexion," Miz Mac said with a lift of her chin.

But she *was* very pale, and she'd evidently applied more rouge in an effort to camouflage it. Though reason told her it was make-up, Rachel was alarmed and laid her hand on her aunt's cheek to feel for fever. She was cool, however. "Aunt Lyddy, you have got to—"

"Now look, girl, just because you're a doctor, don't think you can boss me around."

"I'm not a doctor, Miz Mac," said Nonie, "and I sure think you've been working too hard!"

Rachel swallowed hard and said softly, "Haven't you done enough, at least for today?"

The loving, concerned worry on her niece's face broke down her defenses. Still, she tried. She held up the fine steel wool. "I should at least finish this."

She was standing beside an old oak wash-stand. Rachel took the steel wool from her gently. "Let me do it. You taught me, remember?" she hastened to say as her aunt started to protest. "Now sit down, and you can supervise. Nonie, is there any tea in the ice box?"

"Sure," said Nonie, noticing gratefully that her lifelong friend had slipped into the battered old wicker settee that neither of them could part with. Its worn pale pink chintz cushions were smooth and welcoming, and Miz Mac's head, usually erect when she sat, eased back as she watched Rachel's long, even strokes, with the grain, as she'd taught her.

"I found something this morning that will justify all the work it took for us both to make me a doctor, if I'm right."

"What's that, girl?" came the quiet question. Aunt Lyddy's eyes were closed, and her face was calm and relaxed.

"I think I've found what's causing Lana Beth's problems." Rachel explained and was gratified to see her aunt's eyes open now, and sparkling with shared pleasure.

"That's wonderful! Have you told her yet?"

"In a little while, I'm going in to Houston to do just that."

Miz Mac chuckled. "Think you might find time to call that brown-eyed, curly-headed man...let's see, what was his name?"

"I might." Rachel couldn't repress the tiny smile. She certainly had thought of it. There was no sound in the large, cluttered room for a while, except for the soft

94

whisper of the steel wool smoothing away the last vestiges of old finish.

Realizing she'd been avoiding really looking at her aunt, Rachel forced herself to now, and not as a relative, but as a doctor. What she saw made her throat tighten. There were violet shadows under Lyddy McGeary's eyes, and the tiny blue veins in her closed lids showed through the fine skin. "Aunt Lyddy," she said softly, "you're going to have to be more careful of yourself."

The blue eyes flickered open again. "Girl, part of me knows you're right. And I'm sorry to worry you. But another part of me says if I don't keep going, if I don't ...fight this thing, it'll win. And I'm not going to let that happen."

Still making long, even strokes across the already satin-smooth surface of the washstand, Rachel said slowly, "We just have to work together to find the balance, don't we, though? What's too much, how much you need to do...?" Her voice held a plea.

"Yes." Miz Mac looked at Rachel steadily for a long time. "You've made a fine woman, and you're a fine doctor, too. I didn't do so bad, did I? For an old maid, anyway?"

Rachel dropped the steel wool, quickly covered the distance between them, and sat on the ample, soft seat beside her aunt. Her arms were tight about the thin body as she whispered, "You've been as good a mother as a girl would want—"

There was no answer for a moment, except for a muffled, almost teary one. Lyddy McGeary wasn't a teary woman. She lifted her head suddenly and said, "You'd better get on into the big city and straighten those fellows at the Medical Center out. It's up to you to rescue Lana Beth!"

Her face was lively, animated again, and Rachel caught her close. "If you promise you'll use good sense and listen to your body when it says slow down. Will you?" she asked, allowing the anxiety she felt to show.

"I will." Those clear blue eyes met her niece's, and there was the light of truth in them. "I will, I promise, if you'll tell that good-looking rascal Johnny hello for me, and that I'm feeling neglected because he hasn't been out in a while."

Rachel laughed. "That's *my* line!"

The phone rang then, and Nonie sang out that it was for Miz Mac. Rachel hugged her tight, then left before she gave in to the urge to press her advantage and give out more warnings.

The appointments with Lana Beth and her doctor took less time than she'd anticipated, and Rachel was free by a quarter till five. She found a phone and called Johnny's office, hoping he would still be there. Not only was he still there, he insisted she come over and pick him up. The scratch on his car (that she'd inflicted, he slyly reminded her) was being painted, and he'd taken a cab to work that day.

As she rode up the seventeen floors in the smooth, silent elevator, she glanced down at her dress and admitted that she'd chosen the beautifully blended blue and green and turquoise plaid skirt and blouse for two reasons. It looked like a dress to wear when you felt fall in the air, and she looked very good in it. The wide bateau neckline brought the clean colors near her face. Their richness made her skin look even clearer and tinged her gray eyes with blue-green.

Pleased at the prospect of seeing Johnny in his work environment, Rachel thought that he'd certainly seen her in hers often enough. She felt a curious need to know him in every phase of his life, and she remembered what he'd said about watching her operate.

He was waiting for her now and drew her out of the elevator, his arm possessive around her waist. She met so many people so quickly they were a blur. One thing they all seemed to have in common, however, from the smiling, chic receptionist to Johnny's boss, was a lively curiosity about her. As she and Johnny made a whirlwind tour of the tastefully monochromatic, beige office suite, one other thing emerged clearly: their unanimous, obvious good will toward Johnny.

Johnny was in great spirits, even as he directed her through the snarl of work traffic. "I can't tell you how it tickled me to be able to show you off! Why are you in town, anyway?" He sat in the passenger's seat, his hand on her shoulder, his fingers caressing the smooth fabric of her blouse. "Pretty," he murmured.

Rachel's smile flashed and he saw it, even though she never took her eyes from the melee of five o'clock traffic in Houston. "Where is this fabulous restaurant, and are you absolutely sure we can get there from here?"

"Trust me," he murmured, his fingers warm on her neck.

She laughed outright. "How many times have unsuspecting—or suspecting—females heard that?"

"And fallen for it gladly?" He leaned over and kissed her neck once, twice...a horn sounded behind them. "Get into the left-hand lane—"

"*Now*?" Rachel wailed and made it by the skin of her teeth. By the time she pulled into the restaurant parking lot, they were both laughing for no reason at all except for the sheer pleasure of being together. She looked around and shook her head. "Johnny, this is one of the worst areas in town! The ship channel should be—"

"Right over there," he supplied, getting out and waiting as she came around the car. He watched as she eyed the collection of antique cars displayed there. They were closer to deserted, rusted-out hulks. As if that were not enough, there was clothesline stretched at one side of the rambling old building, and the clothes hanging there consisted of overalls, well-used long johns, and various other things that looked as though a tribe of bachelor miners lived nearby.

"We could get mugged around here, you know."

He pulled open the door, which protested loudly.

"Don't worry, I'll protect you."

Rachel shook her head as she saw what made the heavy, weathered old door work. A huge bucket of rocks hooked up to a pulley contraption made it swing shut behind them. She couldn't resist saying, "How are you going to protect me, you and your broken leg? Hit him with your crutch?"

He grinned. "Sounds like a good plan. Hey, you're going to love this place. We should bring Miz Mac here sometime."

"Why?" asked Rachel, but soon saw why for herself. The walls, every available inch of floor space, the lofts above their heads were covered with relics of the past hundred years. "This is marvelous!"

"I thought you'd like it," Johnny said, after telling their attractive young waitress they'd like a table where they could see the water.

She led them to a table with a remarkably lovely view of the Houston Ship Channel, which is not always considered beautiful. Johnny flashed the waitress a smile and ordered a dinner that she knew would earn her a large tip.

"Johnny, you're the most extravagant man I've ever met!" said Rachel when he'd finally closed the menu and handed it to the young woman.

"Really?" he asked, pleased.

"You act as though you think it's a virtue," she added, a little troubled.

Johnny shrugged. "I guess I do think it's more of a virtue than being stingy, and it's a lot more fun." Obviously anxious to change the subject, he asked, "How'd you like the crew at the office?"

Even though Rachel was still a little disturbed about his cavalier attitude toward money, she was sensitive enough to see he wanted to talk about something else. "I liked them all very much," she said honestly. "But I guess what I liked even more was the way you seem to feel not only about them, but about your job in general."

"What do you mean?"

"Oh, just that it pleases me to see a man who's happy in his work. There are certainly plenty of people in the world who are desperately unhappy in their careers. I've even treated a couple that I'm certain were ill because of dissatisfaction with their jobs."

"I guess I'd have to give my daddy part credit and God part credit for the fact that I ended up as a petroleum geologist."

Rachel's laugh was soft and delighted. "I can understand your father's part in it since he introduced you to oil field work. But what about God?"

Just then the waitress brought a huge platter of fantastic looking hors d'oeuvres, and for a few moments their conversation was sidetracked. Finally Johnny grinned, wiped his mouth carefully, and said, "I didn't have lunch. What's your excuse?"

"Neither did I, but after the breakfast Aunt Lyddy and I had, I didn't need it!" Rachel thought, just at the moment, *He must surely be the most handsome man in the room, the city...maybe the world*. His brown eyes were vitally alive, his tanned, well-shaped face.... She shook herself mentally. "You were telling me how God influenced your career when we were interrupted, I believe."

"Well, I was always a reader. And when I discovered astronomy in high school and began to wonder about how the earth was formed, it wasn't a quantum leap to God's part in it. One thing led to another, and when I also discovered geology, that was it. It's really awesome when you think of how God did it all."

"You don't have any problems with scientific theories and the ideas of God's creation, then?"

"None whatever," he said firmly. "As a geologist I really feel that the earth is a trust, and I want to do what I can to make sure we stop misusing its resources and start preserving what's left." He smiled a little self-consciously. "Enough about my pet causes. You never did tell me why you're in town. Not that it really matters...I'm just glad you're here."

Rachel had her chin in her hand, head to one side. "Remember the woman I admitted at St. Joseph's that first day you met Aunt Lyddy?"

"Hm, yes, I do. How is she?" When Rachel told him what she suspected, he said with satisfaction, "I've been telling you that you're a good doctor."

Her eyes shone. "This is one time I believe I've caught something the others didn't, and she's been to several specialists. It's difficult for them to see the whole person, as I feel we GP's have to try to do. We won't know for sure that it's lupus until we get the results of the tests, but I really believe I'm right."

"I sure don't pretend to know much about it, but it seems that you doctors don't always see eye to eye."

"Its true. I've only been practicing on my own for just over a year, but that's enough to know that a lot of my colleagues look at things far differently from the way I do, or ever will."

"In what ways?" He hitched his chair closer to hers, put his arms on the table and leaned even closer, his dinner forgotten.

His total interest was heady, encouraging stuff. Rachel had often pondered the fact of how few people cared ...really cared about another's dreams and hopes and fears. Johnny seemed to be one of the few who did. Aloud she said, "Oh, just that a great many doctors, young and old—that doesn't seem to matter—are practicing a kind of medicine that isn't right for me. For instance, I'm for progress within reason, but there's so much high tech in medicine now that I really believe it separates us from our patients."

"I've gotten the feeling that some doctors prefer it that way," Johnny said wryly.

"You're right, I suspect. Med school and internship

and residency have a tendency to do that anyway—to put us on a planet apart from other human beings." Thoughtfully she said, "At least the trend is away from thinking of doctors as gods and giving them total power."

Johnny was grinning. "Now me, I never did think of doctors as gods. I'll have to admit, though, that first night when you told me *you* were the doctor, the thought did occur to me that you might be a goddess, if a tee-nincy one!"

"Tee-nincy? I can't remember the last time I heard that!"

He controlled his grin with an effort and tried to look solemn. "The problem is, you live outside the Thicket. Tee-nincy is a perfectly good word, and you're a perfectly good doctor. I could tell that when you were fixing up my leg. Your hands..." He reached over and took both her small hands in his. "They make people feel better. And you care deeply. You're a good doctor," he repeated. Suddenly he said, "Rachel, do you want children? Of your own, I mean?"

Startled, she answered slowly, "I suppose so. Don't most women? What makes you ask that question?"

"Because you're so totally involved with your work, I guess, and because I want to know all about you. Is there room in your life for a husband and children, Rachel?" His brown eyes held hers, and she felt compelled to answer as honestly as she could.

"Yes, I want a home of my own, and a family. But the past ten years have been so full, so demanding, that I just haven't thought much about it."

"That's natural. But when the right man comes along—" He didn't finish that sentence, but he started another even more disturbing one. "What will you do when they're small? Your children, I mean?"

With a slight frown on her face she replied slowly, "I really haven't given it much thought."

"You ought to." He toyed with his spoon for a moment, then added, "I feel that children need their mother...at home full time, with them during those important years. Maybe even all the time they're home."

Several things ran through Rachel's mind. Quality time that a mother spends with her children is what's important, not quantity, children are fine if they have someone to care adequately for their needs, and other similar arguments working women propose in books and articles At the other end of the spectrum there was the quiet insistence that a mother was best qualified, if she allowed God to equip her, to give her own children what they need. Before she could voice any of her thoughts, Johnny spoke again.

"I can't help but admire you, Rachel. You do your job well—I've watched you." He rapped the cast with his knuckles. "I'm living proof of your expertise. You've got healing hands, and you care, really care about people. It's just that I get to wondering if there's room—" He broke off, smiling at the waitress as she presented the check.

Rachel was quiet. She knew the conflict in his mind. It had occurred to her when she'd stopped long enough to think during the past ten years. Was there enough Rachel to be a really good doctor *and* a woman...a wife and mother? It was a question she preferred not to answer at that moment, for she truly didn't know. But she did know that Johnny Allen would not allow her to dodge it forever.

Chapter Nine

Only when she was seeing patients could Rachel keep her thoughts from dwelling on her conversation with Johnny the previous evening. She'd had a full morning at her office and was just making a notation on little Jenny's chart when the phone rang. All her pleasure over the child's remarkable healing fled at the words Willow gasped out. "Oh, Dr. McGeary, there's a man here. He's...I think he's having a a really bad heart attack!"

"All right, Willow. Is Nurse Patt there?"

"Yes, but he's bad, and Dr. Burleigh is in Houston—"

"I'll be right there."

Grateful that no train was blocking the tracks, Rachel made it to the hospital in record time.

The next hour was a nightmare. Despite their best efforts, the man died not long after Rachel reached the hospital. His wife and sixteen-year-old son watched in mute horror as he slipped away. Talking with them was almost as awful for Rachel as losing a patient. Neither the woman nor her son blamed Rachel, and for that she was grateful. But when Anson Burleigh came hurrying in, Rachel knew the ordeal was far from over.

"Tell me exactly what happened," he snapped, his eyes hard and probing.

"Surely, Dr. Burleigh," she began calmly, breathing a

silent prayer that she would use the right words. "He was brought in at 12:37, complaining of pains originating between his shoulder blade earlier in the day, moving to his chest a little later, and—"

"Any tingling in his hands, shortness of breath, cold sweats, complaints of weakness or dizziness?" he barked.

"Yes, to the last three. He had no history of heart disease," she added quickly before he could ask.

"And your diagnosis?"

"Massive coronary thrombosis, sir," Rachel said steadily. "There was nothing more we could have done."

"Just what *did* you do?"

"Miss Willow had given him oxygen and properly attached him to the monitor before I arrived. The defibrillator was—"

"Which you used?"

Rachel nodded, saying tersely, "With no effect. I also tried direct injections into the heart muscle. I...I did everything I felt was indicated." Bone-weary, she wondered why Burleigh always managed to make her feel as though she needed to defend herself.

"And has the family been informed?"

Rachel took a deep breath and said, "His wife and son were present at the moment of death, Dr. Burleigh."

Burleigh's eyes grew even colder. "They were present? That was most unwise."

"Perhaps, but—"

"Dr. McGeary, surely you understand what a trauma it was for the woman and her son to be allowed to witness the death?"

"Yes, of course, but we were trying to save the man's life!"

"At which attempt you were unsuccessful, obviously."

Suddenly Rachel felt overwhelmed. It must have showed in her face, for the older doctor's expression softened a little. "I've no doubt you did the best you could with what you had at your disposal," he said, blue eyes thoughtful now.

"I tried, Dr. Burleigh, I tried." *No tears, Rachel, no tears*, she told herself forcefully.

"Sure you did." He put his arm around her shoulders and hugged her briefly. "But there's something we can't overlook here."

"What's that?" asked Rachel, afraid she knew already.

"If he'd been in Houston, he might be alive at this very moment!" He spoke in a low, dramatic voice now.

"But you can't be certain of that," protested Rachel.

"He's dead," said Burleigh with an eloquent shrug. "And you're forgetting that Houston pioneered heart doctoring. Why, with fellas like DeBakey and ole Denton Cooley, and—"

With a small scowl on her face Rachel said, "I'm not sure Denton Cooley could have done better here today."

"I couldn't have said it better myself, darlin'," Burleigh said triumphantly. "Cooley probably couldn't have...*here*."

"But if we had a coronary care unit, that would help enormously, wouldn't it?"

"It might. But we're operating in the red now, and equipment like you're talking about doesn't grow on trees."

"I'm just not convinced that the usefulness of Marvin Community is at an end," she said stubbornly.

"Even after today?"

"No, not even after today."

"It'll soon be time for our annual board meeting, Rachel. And you know good and well they aren't going to take lightly the fact that we're so far in the red."

"No, they won't," she admitted slowly.

"Well, darlin'," said Dr. Burleigh with a friendly little pat, "why don't you take the rest of the day and evening off? I'll cover for you."

Knowing he was patronizing her, also knowing that

the other patients (all two of them) were his, she nodded. "Thank you, Dr. Burleigh," she said meekly. Inwardly she was seething. She knew if she wasn't careful, he'd win.

She was able to persuade Miz Mac to go out for an early supper, though Rachel barely touched hers. Shortly after they got home, the phone rang.

"How's my girl?"

"Oh, Johnny..." Her throat closed for a moment. She waved to Miz Mac who grinned, rolled her eyes expressively, and headed up the stairs. Rachel nestled in the chair by the window, the phone cradled to her ear.

"Honey, what's wrong?"

His voice was warm, so sympathetic she almost let the tears come. "It's been a rough day. We...I lost a man. He just had a massive coronary and went out in spite of everything we did."

"That's rough." There was a moment of silence, not uncomfortable, then he said, "Need to get away for a while?"

"Do I! But Aunt Lyddy—" Just then she heard her aunt call down, "I'm going to have Nonie over this evening, so if he asks you out, go on!" Smiling and shaking her head, Rachel said, "What do you have in mind?"

"Well, you said you wanted to go see a rodeo, and there's one over at Kountze tonight. We could drive over to Saratoga to a place I know that serves the best food in Texas. It's called Mama's, and I mean, as an eating experience, it's a ten."

"But Johnny, we shouldn't just drop in on your mother—"

"You're right. I'll call, just as soon as I hang up. She'll be glad to see you. She likes you a lot."

Rachel grimaced. "What about your dad?"

"Don't worry about him. Be ready to go in half an hour."

"Don't drive that fast, you nut!" she chided.

"Would you believe me if I told you I was on the way,

that I have a mobile unit in the car?"

"No. Johnny, I..." She trailed off, unwilling to say just how much she needed to see him.

He obviously had no such compunction. "I can't wait to see you, Doc."

She hesitated only a fraction of a second before she said, "Me, too. Bye."

Rachel took a deep breath. The air was laden with rich odors: horses and cattle and straw, hot dogs and candy apples and barbecue from the carnival that always accompanied the rodeo. She turned to Deenie, who sat beside her on the wooden bleachers as they waited for the grand entry. "It looks as though we've been deserted, doesn't it?"

"Not for the first time," replied Deenie serenely. When Dolly had begged to stay at the carnival with a group of girlfriends, Deenie had reluctantly said yes. Rachel suspected her reluctance was largely due to the fact that Joe Bob had come up just then and joined them. Rachel told herself it was none of her business and turned to watch Johnny, who, with Joe Bob, was making his stiff-legged way around the arena to the time booth above the bucking chutes. They'd asked him— over the crackly loud-speakers—to help keep time, and he'd eagerly accepted.

"Deenie, has Johnny always enjoyed rodeos?"

The older woman nodded, smoothing the full skirt of her denim dress. "He always liked horses, at any rate. Now, Jim, he'd rather go hunting, the way he did tonight."

Rachel knew Deenie had asked him to come with them, but he refused, saying he and some of his buddies had a coon hunt planned. She tried to think of a tactful way to bring up the other subject on her mind. "Dolly told me about your antiques business. I just want you to know I admire you and agree with you totally."

"Agree with what?" But Deenie was not looking at Rachel. The grand entry was beginning, and a man bearing the U.S. flag galloped past on a beautiful bay. Deenie and Rachel, along with everyone else in the bleachers, rippled to their feet. "Oh, look!" Deenie cried. "They've got the little Bradshaw boy on a horse! Why, he can't be four yet—"

Fascinated and a little fearful, Rachel watched as the tot galloped past. The stirrups on the tiny saddle he sat couldn't have been a foot long. He wore an enormous black hat, pulled low on his head. "He's darling," said Rachel, delighted. "Did Johnny ride that young?"

"No, we never had the money for a horse," Deenie replied.

Which brought Rachel back to what they'd been talking about earlier. "Dolly tells me you're a fine businesswoman, that you've got enough saved to put her through at least the first two years of college."

"Dolly talks too much."

Rachel heard the affection in the abrupt statement. "She's a lovely girl, Deenie. She deserves the chance to go to school. Are you...when do you plan to tell Jim? About the money, I mean, and Dolly's college plans?" When Deenie didn't reply immediately, Rachel said, "I'm sorry. You're probably thinking this is none of my business."

"No, I'm not thinking that at all." Deenie sat down, her eyes on Johnny up in the time booth. He waved, and she waved back. Then she said, "There's been lots of times I wanted to talk about things to another woman." She turned to face Rachel now. "As for when I plan to let Jim in on my little business venture...to tell you the truth, I hadn't planned that far ahead. I just had to do something to give Dolly a better chance than—"

"Than you had, maybe?"

Deenie shook her head. "Don't get me wrong. I've had the life I wanted. Jim, the kids—making a home for people you love is pretty important."

"That's certainly true. Oh, look!" The little cowboy was flying by, one hand on his fourteen-gallon hat, the other clutching his pommel. Rachel glanced at Deenie. "And you never felt as though you missed anything by not having a career?"

Deenie's smile was gentle. "Rachel, I *have* a career. Sometimes more than I can handle. And I don't just mean my little antiques business. I am a full-time homemaker. My family has had the best there is in me."

The proud, yet somehow humble look on Deenie's face awed Rachel. "Don't you ever get tired of the way he...lords it over you, expects you to wait on you hand and foot?"

Again, that smile. "Mostly, no."

"But he acts as though he thinks he's better than you are, *superior*!"

Deenie laughed now. "He does, doesn't he?"

"The Bible says we're equal, Deenie."

"Not to a Thicket man, hon." Deenie sobered now, and after a moment she said slowly, "In my heart I know the Lord loves me just the same as he does Jim or any other man who ever walked around in pants. And I know we're equal in His sight. But I still have to live in the circumstances I'm dealt."

"What does that mean?" Rachel asked, confused.

"Just that the things Jim asks and expects of me don't hurt me. I like doing things for people I love. Being a servant isn't a bad thing, like people make it out." Her eyes twinkled. "Jesus sure did plenty of it."

"Yes," said Rachel, a little frown still on her face. "But to me, being equal means being partners. Sharing responsibilities and burdens, being honest with each other." Too late, she realized Deenie might think she was talking about her secret business.

"If you're wondering whether I feel bad not telling Jim about the money and our plans, I do."

"Oh, I didn't mean..."

"It's all right. I know it's not honest of me. But I want

things to be right for Dolly so bad."

"You shouldn't have to do it secretly."

Deenie's chin lifted proudly. "It'll work out. And after it's all said and done, Jim'll be proud. He'll probably say the whole thing was his idea."

Rachel smiled. She'd never known anyone like the woman who sat beside her. A woman who was intelligent and thoughtful, and even in a situation which Rachel would have found intolerable, acted in a way that was totally consistent with her beliefs as a Christian. Aloud all she said was, "I like your kitchen, Deenie."

Deenie's smile said it all—she knew Rachel understood her. Something real and warm had begun between them. "The roping is starting. Breakaway first, tie-down next." They spied Johnny just then, making his stiff-legged way toward them.

He flopped beside Rachel. "Joe Bob drew José. He's a mighty good bull, and I decided it'd be a lot more fun sitting close to you and telling you how much better I could do it if wasn't for this bum pin." He smiled at her, his arm slipping around her waist. "Or maybe I could just go ahead and ride, take my chances."

"John Wesley Allen, don't even talk about it!" his mother scolded.

Rachel put her arm around his waist and pulled tight, glad for an excuse to be close to him. "I've got him, Deenie, and I'm not letting go."

A speculative look filled Deenie's eyes as she surveyed them. "Good," was all she said.

For the remainder of the rodeo Johnny gave a full commentary on each event, complete with a rundown on each cowboy's life story. When it came time for the bull-riding event, he got a little wistful.

"See, hon, Joe Bob's behind chute number three. Ol José is one mean ton of bull," said Johnny.

Rachel knew the tiny, regretful sigh at the end of his words was because it was Joe Bob, not him, who was waiting for the gate to open. She could see the huge brindle bulk of the bull between the slats. Joe Bob's boot toes were hooked under the top one, above the bull's back, and common sense told her that was to keep from being crushed if 'ol José' should decide to slam against the wall of the chute. "I'm afraid he'll be hurt...."

"Nah," said Johnny nonchalantly, but he tensed a little as the announcer bawled out, "And now, coming out of chute number three is one of our own, Joe Bob Connor!"

Rachel couldn't resist tapping his cast. "Cowboys don't ever get hurt, hm?"

"I just hope he's got a real hold on that bull rope," Johnny muttered, ignoring the little dig.

"Bull rope?" questioned Rachel.

"It's looped round the bull's body, then round Joe Bob's hand," said Johnny, his attention riveted on chute number three. "One hand, that's all the contact he's allowed, except the seat of his britches. Helps him stay on, hopefully, or—"

Just then the bull exploded into the arena to the tune of a great shout from the stands. Flinging himself forward, his huge body contracting and stretching like an accordian during a polka, the bull made a spiraling motion, a sort of roll and twist. His pelvis rolled one way, his front twisted the other; then he reversed the spine-cracking motion.

"Sunfishing," muttered Johnny, his voice low, his eyes on Joe Bob.

"What's that?" said Rachel, awed as her doctor's eye saw the punishment to Joe Bob's flesh and bones.

For a moment Johnny didn't speak. Then the horn blew, signifying that Joe Bob had ridden the full time—eight seconds—and well, too. "Good ride," he said, relief obvious in his tone. Then he added, "Haven't you ever caught a little old perch and had him flop from side to side, twisting like that?"

"I guess so," said Rachel, searching her memory, then nodding slowly. "Yes, I can see why they call it sunfishing."

The bull, freed of his aggravating burden, ignored Joe Bob, who strutted toward the fence, one eye still peeled to make sure the brute wasn't after him.

Rachel heard Deenie sigh. "I'm just glad it wasn't you on that beast, Johnny."

Her son's sigh matched hers, but his was from another source entirely...envy. "Good ride, good ride."

As they were leaving a little later Dolly came up with Joe Bob Connor trailing behind her, her hand in his. "Look who I found, Mama," she said brightly.

Deenie smiled back, but it was strained. "I thought you were with your friends, Dolly."

"Joe Bob is my friend, Mama," Dolly replied, instantly on the defensive. "Wasn't he great?"

"Yes, he sure was." Deenie must have decided to meet the situation head on. "Joe Bob, why don't you come over to the house and have some strawberry rhubarb pie to celebrate that ride?"

"I'd love to, Mrs. Allen, but—" Joe Bob stopped, but Deenie read his mind.

"Jim's gone coon hunting tonight. Did Johnny tell you?" she asked offhandedly.

The change on Joe Bob's face was almost comical. "No, he didn't. Say, I like a good coon hunt myself. I just might come over for a spell. Can I give you a ride?"

His sunburnt, snub-nosed face was open and honest, and Deenie smiled at him. "That's a good idea. You can take Dolly and me, 'cause I've got a notion these two—" she nodded at Rachel and Johnny, "might want to take the long way home."

"Sounds good," said Johnny, who still had his hand around Rachel's waist. "We'll see you at the house. I might show Rachel the Old Bragg Road."

"Hey, buddy, see you later," said Joe Bob as he respectfully stood aside for Dolly and her mother. "Mrs. Allen, I appreciate the invitation."

"Call me Deenie, Joe Bob." Deenie took one of the young man's arms.

Dolly, her face relaxed and happy, caught Joe Bob's other arm, and he strutted off between them.

For a while Rachel didn't speak as they walked in the milling crowd. Then she said slowly, "Your mother is a smart woman."

"I sure can agree with that," Johnny said. "But what makes you say so now?"

"Didn't you see what she just did? Joe Bob is dead serious about Dolly, and your mother knows it."

"Sure, I know it, too. But Dolly is too young to know what kind of man she wants."

"That's probably true," admitted Rachel. "But your mother's smart enough to realize that if Dolly rebels against...."

"My daddy?" Johnny supplied.

She nodded. "You know it's a possibility. Deenie knows it, too, and rather than confront him about it, she chose to defuse the situation by making Joe Bob welcome. Johnny, Dolly could do worse than Joe Bob."

Johnny scowled as he opened her car door. "She could do a whole lot better, too." He closed it behind her and made his way around to the driver's side, got in, and sat for a moment. "I think I know how the folks feel. Both of them, in their own ways, want what's best for her." He started the engine and drove a little too fast as they left the rodeo grounds. "Being an only child the way you were and not having any kids of your own yet, I can't really see how you're any kind of authority, even if you are a doctor." He drove in silence for a couple of miles and the lights of the small community were soon behind them.

Stung by his curt, if undeniable, statement, she thought carefully before she answered. "You're right, of course. But doesn't it seem as though the main job of parents is to raise their children to know how to make their own decisions? And if you haven't done that by the time they're as old as Dolly is, something's wrong."

Once again he was silent as the close, dark woods on either side of the narrow state road blurred past. Then he said, "This is awful hard on me, Rachel. It seems like you're always attacking my folks."

"Oh, Johnny, is that how you see it?" she cried.

"What else would you call it?"

His quiet, hard question pierced her heart. "Please forgive me. I didn't realize...I never thought of it like that. It's just that I like you all very much. Your whole family is...I guess what I'm trying to say is, I already care about them." She paused, then added softly, "You said it yourself a while back, I was raised differently, just Aunt Lyddy and me. Forgive me, please?"

He eased the car onto a gravelly turn-off, cut the lights and the engine, then put a hand on her shoulder. "Sure, honey. Hey, how'd we get this serious, anyhow?" He pulled her close and kissed the edge of her ear.

Rachel shivered, feeling her insides turn to jelly. Breathlessly she said, "Tell me about the Bragg Road ghost light....I assume there's a tale involved?"

His lips brushed her jaw. "More than one. I've heard the light described as hot, as cold, as floating, leaping, stationary, sometimes red, white, blue, green or combinations of all of the above." He buried his face in her hair. "Your hair smells like honeysuckle. I love honeysuckle."

It wasn't easy for Rachel to speak. Her breath seemed completely gone now. "Does it...does the light ever chase people?"

He drew back a little, trying to see her face in the dimness. The windows of the car were down, and the night sounds drifted in—crickets and multitudes of croaking frogs. From the distance an owl's cry pierced the darkness. "As a matter of fact, during one period of time there was some talk about it chasing cars. One fella said it even got on top of his car and tromped around."

She giggled. "Do you believe those tales?"

With a shrug of his shoulders he said, "The scientists say it's just low grade gas, commonly found in swampy areas, especially since this is an old oil field."

"Gas! Ah, that takes all the romance out of it," objected Rachel softly, yielding to the gentle pressure of his arm that drew her closer again.

"I wouldn't say that. Why do you think I brought you here? Bragg Road has always been a lovers lane."

"I see..." The words were faint, blurred by the touch of Johnny's lips on hers.

It started as a sweet, gentle kiss. Rachel felt lost in the sweetness of it, gave herself gladly to its gentleness. But then, it changed slowly, subtly, to something far different, and she was stirred so deeply that she wanted desperately to be closer. She pressed herself against him tighter.

Johnny broke away, and though he still held her tightly, his hand was at the back of her head, pressing it to his shoulder. "Rachel, sweetheart."

The sound of her name cleared the fever in her brain. She murmured, "You must think I'm...I'm not—"

"Doc," he said, holding her as a man might hold his little girl—close, but protective. "I'll tell you exactly what I think of you. I think you're the most beautiful, the warmest, the most exciting woman God ever made. I feel—"

"I know what you feel!"

He laughed, "Yeah, I guess you do!" He held her at arm's length for a moment, then caught her close again. "And isn't it the neatest thing going? Hey, don't you know that's something a man dreams about, a woman who's as stirred by him as he is by her? It's just that I think a woman ought not to—"

"Show it?" she interrupted faintly.

He shook his head. "That's not what I was going to say at all. I was going to say that a woman ought not to have the whole job of, um...keeping things on an even keel. You are some kind of woman, Doc, and I could get plumb carried away."

"But you didn't."

His fingers traced the line of her jaw, tenderly rounded the edge of her ear. "Rachel, I'm no psychologist, but I'd say that what happened today, that man dying, I mean, has something to do with all this."

"Oh?" She had an idea what he was about to say.

"I've got a notion that seeing someone die shook you up mighty bad. And made you vulnerable. To me, to your own feelings about me."

Rachel wanted to tell him she'd been vulnerable to him before today, but she didn't. "You're right, of course. It was a shock. I can never see someone die without it affecting me deeply."

"Any good doctor, or anyone, for that matter, should feel the same. And as for this Burleigh creep—"

"Johnny!" she chided. "Let's just say he didn't make it easier for me."

"Like I said, he's a creep," Johnny repeated cheerfully. "And I'd have been one, too, if I'd allowed myself to take advantage of you when you're so vulnerable."

Rachel was beginning to realize how very precious a gift Johnny had just given her. She drew a shaky breath. "Thank you."

"For what?" He kissed her softly just to the left of her mouth.

"You know for what. Johnny, I've never had these kinds of feelings, not like this, for anyone else."

"I'm glad." His lips moved to her mouth, but he kissed her lightly, almost chastely. "We'd better go now. I might lose the next round."

"And I'm no help." Suddenly she tightened her arms around him and clasped him almost fiercely. "Oh, Johnny, I—" She stopped, the words she was about to say sticking in her throat.

"It's okay. There's time." He started the engine, but before he pulled out onto the road he added, "Not much, but there's time."

Chapter Ten

The first few months after Rachel had renovated and reopened her father's office she'd found herself spending mornings rearranging things, taking long lunch hours, and reading medical journals in the afternoons, with only an occasional patient to break the monotony. Gradually word had gotten around. *Dr. McGeary takes time to really explain things...Dr. McGeary listens...Dr. McGeary is kind....*

Things were certainly no longer quiet and monotonous. As Rachel breathed deeply for what felt like the first time that day and checked her appointment book, she was pleased to find she'd seen her last patient. It had been a very good day, and Lana Beth Duvall's surprise visit had added immeasurably to Rachel's sense that "all's right with the world." Lana Beth's gratitude that she finally could put a name to her illness—systemic lupus erythematosus—knew no bounds.

And Sandy Bailey's decision to have her baby at home was an exciting prospect....

Just then there was a knock at the door. "Come in," she called. It was Johnny, his brown eyes pleased at her look of delight. "Johnny, what in the world are you doing here?" She rose and went to meet him, walking gladly into his outstretched arms.

He hugged her tightly. "I had to see you."

"But why?"

Instead of answering, he kissed her. "That's why. Ready for supper?"

"As a matter of fact, I am. How'd you like to try Frank's? He has good seafood—"

"How about a sumptuous repast from the Brass Plum, the place where all the 'little River Oaks housewives,' as Stan calls them, go?"

"That sounds marvelous, but I'm not sure I can last that long."

"I didn't mean go into Houston. I brought it with me. The picnic extraordinaire. Where's the best place to have it?"

"Aunt Lyddy's yard is nicer than any park, and there's a table. I hate eating on the ground."

"Good. She can eat with us. There's plenty." He was herding her out the door as he spoke.

A little smile curved her mouth. "We'll be alone. She and Nonie had a rush order."

"What a shame." He winked at her, his eyes merry. "How's she doing these days, anyway?"

Rachel rested her head on the seat as he started off. "She really is doing pretty well. I just think she works too hard...like this evening."

"You ought to take a little of your own advice." Johnny pulled up at the train crossing and cut his engine. The slow moving freight train that blocked their way looked about sixty miles long.

"Meaning?" she asked, though she suspected she knew.

"Meaning you have to let Miz Mac make her own choices, her own decisons about her illness. Remember all that talk about letting kids go after they're grown? It goes for grown-up relatives and friends, too, you know."

"I guess you're right. But I'd rather talk about the good day I had today."

"So talk," Johnny said, brushing her cheek with his fingers.

Of course she told him about Lana Beth first. Rachel was still talking about Sandy and Mark Bailey as they settled back on the lawn chairs in Miz Mac's back yard after devouring the elegant picnic he'd brought. "And so they finally compromised. She's going to have the baby at home, and he's going to help."

"But you'll be there," Johnny said, fascinated. "What about getting a midwife? Aren't there any around here?"

"Not that I'm aware of," said Rachel, her hands trailing on either side of the low chair. The sun had gone down only a few moments before, but the air was still hot. The ancient pecan trees provided a welcome protective bower.

"When's she due?"

Rachel sat up. "Any time now. Actually, I suspected today that she could be in the first stages of labor. But it's her first, and it's hard to tell. Her mother has told her so many horror stories I have to be careful not to alarm her."

"What kind of horror stories?" Johnny was massaging his leg. Rachel had removed the cast a few days before and pronounced it fine, but he kept saying it felt strange.

"Oh, when her mother was having babies it was standard practice to drug women heavily, and the babies were taken by instruments at the obstetricians' convenience. She came to Sandy's regular checkup one day, full of fears for her only daughter. Something she said really made an impression on me."

"What's that?" He was gazing down at her.

"She said...'all our babies came smelling of ether, sleepy and bruised, their heads dented like windfallen fruit.' "

"That sounds awful."

"It must have been. At any rate, Sandy's husband has agreed to a home birth."

"But only if you're there." She nodded, eyes closed in complete relaxation. "I don't blame the poor guy for dragging his feet. I'd be scared, too, if it was my wife." Something in his voice made Rachel's eyes fly open. He was looking into them now as he said quietly, "I didn't just come out to bring supper tonight. I've been thinking a lot about things...about us." Their chairs were very close. He reached out for her hand and held it tightly, then sat up and put both feet on the ground. "Rachel, I don't think we can put if off any longer."

"What, Johnny?" She felt suspended. It was a delightful heady sensation, for she knew what he was about to say.

"I want—" The sound of the telephone, jangling on the brick patio nearby interrupted him. Johnny groaned, "Can't we just let it ring, just this once?"

She gave him a quick kiss on her way up. "You know I can't. What if it was Aunt Lyddy...or Sandy?" She caught it on the third ring.

He watched as she asked a few terse questions, then hung up. Resigned, he got up and went over to her. "It's that girl's baby, isn't it?"

"How did you know?"

He touched her cheek. "The look on your face. If it was Miz Mac or something bad, you wouldn't look so excited, so pleased. I'll drive you there."

"Thanks," she replied, already moving inside.

He followed, filled with a mixture of pride and exasperation. At the Bailey house he walked her to the door. "You're really looking forward to this, aren't you?"

She glanced up at him. "Yes, I am. Somehow...it feels right. Oh, Johnny, I know change comes hard, and I want to make sure the changes are good ones. I don't want to go backward."

Johnny shook his head, laughing a little. "Rachel, sweetheart, don't you worry about it." He would have kissed her right then and there, but the door opened to reveal a nervously smiling Mark Bailey. He looked very young, and his sandy hair was standing up in spikes as though he'd run his fingers through it a hundred times.

Rachel smiled at him. "She's going to be fine, Mark. Tell me how it's going." She barely nodded as Johnny patted her shoulder and murmured, "Call me when you want a ride home." He stood a moment, watching Rachel continue to listen closely to Mark, then left.

Inside Rachel felt the excitement in the air. Sandy's mother waved from the kitchen, and when Rachel saw that the woman was carefully placing a candle in the middle of a cake, she chuckled. "What's this, a birthday cake for the first grandchild?"

"You got it." The woman, whose face belied her forty-five years, looked critically at the cake, smoothed a wrinkle of frosting, then said to Rachel. "My baby is doing things differently from the way I did." She glanced over at Sandy, who sat in a large, high-backed rocker, her feet on a little needlepoint footstool. The young woman's face bore a look of intense concentration, and she was watching the clock, hands on her belly.

"Lasted a little over a minute, and they're just under three minutes apart, Dr. McGeary," she said a little breathlessly.

"How bad is the pain, Sandy?" asked Rachel.

"Oh, I'm not going to tell you it doesn't hurt, but it's nothing I can't manage...so far." She grinned, her pretty face lighting up for a moment.

"She's doing great," said Mark, going to stand by her side. His face showed the strain he felt, but to his credit he said nothing in the next half hour that was not totally supportive. The four of them had a cup of tea and a pleasant, if watchful, visit. But when Sandy gave a little gasp, he croaked, "What is it, honey, what's wrong?"

"It's...I think it's almost time," she said, her voice small but excited.

"Help her into the bedroom, Mark, and see that she's comfortable." Rachel watched as he tenderly helped Sandy to her feet, grateful for Sandy's mother's tense silence. She had agreed with no arguments when Sandy had decided that only Mark and Rachel be in the room during the actual birth. Sandy, a young woman who had a clearer insight into herself than most women her age, had said, "If you're there, Mom, I'm afraid I'll revert to being your little girl again, instead of being the new mom!"

In the small bedroom the bed was white and inviting, the sheets taut and clean. Sandy, looking a bit flushed now, said suddenly, "Oh, Dr. McGeary, it feels as though I'm going to explode!"

When Rachel checked she grinned. "You sort of did, Sandy, your waters have broken!"

Several tense moments passed. Then Sandy said, "I feel the head coming down....*Mark*?"

"I'm here; I'm here," he said, one hand on her forehead, the other clutching hers.

Sandy gave a little moan. "It's coming...."

"Yes," Rachel said, "it is!" Rachel supported the baby's head and told Sandy to push when she was ready.

Awed, Mark Bailey watched as Rachel caught the baby. "It's a girl, honey. We have a little girl!" All the anxiety was gone from Mark's voice now. The joy on his face had wiped it away. "She's perfect, isn't she, Dr. McGeary?"

"As far as I can tell, she is absolutely perfect," Rachel said, "and I believe there's someone right outside who'd like to know that."

"Mom!" Mark shouted. "Where are you? You have a granddaughter!"

She must have been just outside the door, for she appeared at once, a little hesitant. But the joy on her face was the same as on her son-in-law's face. "Is Sandy all right?"

"I'm fine, Mom," said Sandy, "just fine." Her mother

came and knelt by the side of the bed.

"Thank God you're all right," she whispered. "I got to thinking maybe we were wrong, maybe you should have gone to the hospital...what if something had gone wrong?"

"Dr. McGeary is here, and it didn't. Look at her...." The baby was lying on Sandy's abdomen, pink and beautiful, making soft little lip-smacking noises.

Rachel cleaned the rosy baby up, wrapped her in a tiny blanket, and put her to the radiant girl's breast. It was close to an hour before the placenta came, and Rachel sat with the little family, delighted to be sharing the birthday cake of Tamara Ilene Bailey. When she'd checked mother and baby one last time, she called Johnny, who answered Aunt Lyddy's phone sleepily.

But he came immediately, his eyes full of unasked questions as they got into the car. Rachel's face told the story even before she began to speak. "It's a girl, she's perfect, and Sandy was wonderful. Even the father is doing fine! Oh, Johnny, it was so...so..." She faltered, unable to express her feelings.

It had indeed been a new experience for her, totally different from all her other deliveries. She thought suddenly that the very word *delivery* was one key. She'd delivered several women of their babies in her short time as a physician, but tonight had been a first. She laughed.

"What's so funny?"

"Do you remember that scene in *Gone with the Wind*, when Prissy says, 'Oh, Miss Scahlett, I doan know nothin' 'bout birthin' babies'?"

"Yes."

"Well, tonight, I didn't deliver that baby, Sandy birthed her!"

"You'll pardon me if I don't catch the fine points, though. It's late. Or early."

"Oh, Johnny," she said, immediately contrite, "you should have gone on home."

"And miss all this? Not on your life. Now explain the difference between delivery and birthing, if you please."

"You're really interested, aren't you?" she asked, both surprised and, indeed, pleased.

He nodded. "Someday I'm going to be in that man's shoes, and I don't want to be totally ignorant. I will let you wait till we get to Miz Mac's to start the lecture, though," he said. "I had a hard time getting her to give up and go to sleep last night. She kept wanting to talk. By the way, I fixed a snack for you. Bet you're hungry, aren't you?"

"I sure am. A snack. And you got Aunt Lyddy to go to bed at a reasonable hour? What have you done, appointed yourself the guardian of the McGeary women?"

"Any objections?"

"I...no, I guess not. What's my snack? I'm starved."

"Birthing babies is hard work, hm?" He wheeled into Miz Mac's driveway and cut the engine. "Well, I'm no cook, but I thought you'd need a little something, so I made nachos. I'm afraid I didn't realize they'd be closer to breakfast than a midnight snack." He grimaced.

"Sounds marvelous to me." As they got out, Rachel stretched enormously, reaching for the sky. Later out on the patio she was stretching yet again when Johnny came out and joined her. She laughed. "After that so-called snack, I need to do calisthenics." Johnny's idea of a snack was enough nachos to feed a Mexican family of sixteen. "Thank you. It was wonderful having someone waiting for me, someone who's interested in...." She started to say, in me, and changed her mind. "In what I'm doing. Especially someone who makes good nachos," she added impishly.

"Speaking of being interested in what you do, you were going to tell me about birthing babies." He came up behind her and began to massage her shoulders.

"Oh, that feels good." She hesitated—it was difficult

to think at this hour of the morning. "Well, I suppose on one hand there's the concept of medical management of pregnancy and delivery, and on the other, working with and helping a woman birth her own babies."

"Doesn't sound as though there's any contest between those two philosophies to me."

"Believe me, there is." Rachel pressed the small of her back. "It's actually a matter of control."

"How's that?" he said, his hands gently rubbing her back.

"Who's in charge, who has control of the situation— the mother-to-be or the doctor? It's all tied together, and it's a matter of emphasis, of attitude. Is it a medical circumstance, an illness to be managed, or a natural happening?"

"That seems obvious to me." He grinned. "But what do I know? Obviously I never gave birth."

"Obviously."Rachel leaned against him. "But one day the woman you love might...." All of a sudden she found she'd lost her objectivity.

"I hope so," he said quietly. "I want children very much, Rachel."

"I...so do I." After tonight, she knew she did, very much, want babies. She also knew she wanted those babies to be hers and Johnny Allen's.

He turned her to face him, his hands on her shoulders. "You are something else, you know that?"

"You said that once before and never got around to explaining." Rachel slipped her arms around his waist. Why was it that she never felt the slightest compunction against reaching out to this man—touching him? The experience with Sandy and Mark Bailey—and little Tamara Ilene—had been heady enough, but sharing it all with Johnny added a dimension she knew had been missing before. She needed him in so many ways.

"Ah, Rachel." His fingers twined in her hair, moving in the soft, warm strands.

"That feels good. My head...the pins hurt sometimes."

He pulled them out one at a time and let them fall to the bricks at their feet. Her hair didn't tumble down all at once. It moved slowly, and he ran his fingers through it until it finally covered her shoulders and trailed down her back. He'd been right when he saw her in the emergency room that first time. Her hair did reach her waist. He buried his face in it. "I love you," he breathed. "You know that I love you, don't you?"

"Yes...." It was more a sigh than a word, but he heard it and caught her close as she said, "I love you, too, Johnny."

The time that followed as they lost themselves in the awesome realization could have been seconds or much longer. Neither really knew. But when Johnny finally said, "Rachel, will you marry me?" she laughed, a clear, lovely sound in the early morning air. He stared at her. "What is this, woman? I ask the question that has never crossed my lips before, and you laugh?"

"Oh, Johnny, what else can I do when I'm so happy? Of course we have to get married. Believe me, the way I feel about you needs legalizing!"

He laughed too, now, and they held each other tight. "I got to thinking while you were at Bailey's that we were probably going to watch another sunrise together, and I decided that was something I'd like to do for the rest of my life, watch the sun come up with you."

With her back close to his chest, Rachel gloried in the warm strength of his arms as they saw the dawn's pale beginning in the sky. For a long time they stood, until the paleness turned to coral, then pearly pink. A mockingbird had been singing for quite a while. It was the sweetest sound she could imagine. It occurred to her that for the rest of her life she would remember that God's best bird (according to an awful lot of Texans) had made the music for her proposal. "It's so beautiful."

"You're beautiful." He turned around and placed a

hand on either side of her face. "I may as well tell you right now, I don't want a long engagement."

The smile on Rachel's mouth was slow and sweet. "Neither do I, Johnny. Neither do I."

He caught her close again, his voice exultant as he said, "Maybe we ought to go down and wake up the JP right now!"

"I need a little more time than that! I want a beautiful dress, and Aunt Lyddy and your family and all our friends with us. And I want to be married in the church here in Marvin. There's a wonderful stained glass window that's radiant when the sun shines through. We'll have to be married at five in the evening."

"Five in the evening? I never heard of a wedding then."

"Well, ours will be," said Rachel definitely. "Because that's when the sun lights that window."

"I don't care what time, just so it's soon."

"It will be, Johnny, I promise."

He took a deep breath, then exhaled in a sigh. "I have to go. Believe me, I don't want to. I don't ever want to leave you again."

"I know." She nestled in his arms, then stood on tiptoe and kissed his mouth lightly. "So go, and call me sometime today so we can compare notes."

"On what?"

She pushed him away. "On how long we can stand it before we have to see each other again, probably."

After one last, lingering kiss, he did reluctantly leave Rachel standing dreamily on the patio, wondering if her face could break from smiling, hoping Aunt Lyddy would wake up early so she could tell her the news.

Chapter Eleven

All of the pieces of Burleigh's puzzling behavior fell into place when Nurse Patt told Rachel about the clinic. It certainly had been a well-kept secret, but since the contractor had broken ground this morning, the entire town was buzzing with the news. Anson Burleigh and his son Sydney, newly graduated from Stanford, were going to work together on the new venture.

"And all that talk about how the hospital wasn't meeting the needs of the community was a smoke screen! Oh, Patt, he can't do this!" wailed Rachel as they sat in the nurses' station at Marvin Community, coffee mugs before them.

"He can, and he's going to." Nurse Patt studied her young friend's distraught face. "It's not like you to be against what could benefit the people of Marvin, and a modern, well-equipped clinic certainly would, even with Burleigh running it."

Rachel's wide gray eyes were as cold as a winter day. "You know me better than that! Of course I'm glad there'll be better care available, and Burleigh is certainly competent. What makes me so mad I can't see straight is how all this time he's been undermining this hospital! Don't you see, without the competition of Marvin Community, his clinic is sure to do well."

"That's probably true."

Rachel shook her head. "I just hate to think he's that money-oriented, Patt."

"He hasn't always been. But things are different now, since he remarried. His new wife just isn't like Maudie was. And his son...if half what they say about the girl *he* married is true, Marvin is in for a social upheaval."

Feeling a tug of conscience, Rachel realized they were edging over into gossip. "Oh, Patt, that's really beside the point. Anson Burleigh has a lot of influence in this town. If he wants to close the hospital for whatever reasons, there's a good chance he can."

"He's got some solid reasons on his side," Nurse Patt said, her face troubled.

"I know." Rachel hunched miserably on the stool, her hands around the cooling mug. "The doors of the patients' rooms aren't up to code, so there's no Medicare or Medicaid. We don't have a coronary care unit, and supplies are always short. I could go on and on. But it all takes money to remedy."

"A lot of money," murmured Patt as she glanced down the hall to see if any lights were on. "Have you seen Julia Briggs today?"

Rachel nodded. "We really need to watch her closely. I don't like the sound of those rales." For a moment Rachel was silent, a tiny furrow between her eyes. "You know, it's patients like Julia that make me so determined to keep the hospital open. If we could bring this hospital up to code so we'd be eligible for Medicare or Medicaid, a lot more people would benefit."

"Now you're really talking big bucks," said Patt with a little whistle. "Have you thought about praying for the money?"

Rachel glanced at her friend's face and saw the teasing glint there. Her chin lifted. "As a matter of fact I have, but I might have to do a lot more before this is all over. The board meeting is next Wednesday, and Burleigh's son is supposed to be there." A little sigh escaped her lips.

"Remembering your flaming affair with him?" Patt chuckled and watched Rachel's face closely.

"Don't call it that! We only had two dates!"

"Tuck your bottom lip in, Doctor. It makes you look seven years old when you pooch it out like that. Say," she said, enormously pleased with Rachel's stormy response, "speaking of flaming affairs, how's it going with the good-looking bronc buster?"

Rachel's eyes became soft and dreamy. "He...Johnny proposed last night—this morning, I guess it was."

"This morning, hm?" asked Patt with a knowing grin.

"Oh, it wasn't like that at all. Sandy Bailey's baby was born last night and I was over there until late, or early, however you want to say it. Johnny picked me up afterward."

"So you're getting married," said Patt fondly. "I'm really glad. When's the date?"

"We aren't sure, but soon, I think. Aunt Lyddy says we need time to at least—" She halted as Patt craned her neck, looking down the hall past her shoulder.

"Here she comes now. She's something else, isn't she?" The affection in her voice was plain. They both watched Miz Mac approach. Her dress was raspberry pink, and her headdress today was a perky matching cloche. As she drew near, Patt shook her head admiringly. "Miz Mac, you look terrific."

"Well, Patt, a woman has to look her best when she goes to the doctor, doesn't she?" Her keen blue eyes sought Rachel's. "We've got to talk, girl."

Rachel knew she hadn't come to talk about wedding plans. "You've heard about Burleigh's plans for the clinic."

"I heard, but I wasn't really too surprised. Burleigh has always looked out for himself." Aunt Lyddy took a long look around. "Things *are* getting kind of tatty around here."

"But Aunt Lyddy—"

The older woman interrupted, waving for Rachel to

follow as she moved away from the nurses' station. "We've got some talking to do, Patt. Okay to use one of the rooms?"

"Seventeen's fine," said Patt, grinning.

"By the way, Patt," she added casually, "I've got a gentleman friend coming to get me in a while."

Patt's eyebrows went up, high. "A gentleman friend? Lyddy McGeary, after all these years—"

"Juanita Maria Patterson, pull in your antennae! Stan Janek is just a friend, nothing more. And bring him in when he comes." She turned and sailed off down the hall toward number 17.

"Sure, Miz Mac, anything you say."

Again Rachel heard the affection in her voice. "Call me if anything comes up." At Nurse Patt's emphatic nod she followed her aunt into 17 and perched on the militarily precise bed in front of her.

Aunt Lyddy didn't waste time getting to the point. "Burleigh has a lot going for him, you know that."

"Yes, he does. But I believe with all my heart that he's wrong about closing the hospital, Aunt Lyddy."

"I think so, too." Miz Mac's eyes were dark and serious. "I also think some of his underlying reasons include prejudice against you because you're a woman. If you'd been a man and the son of his friend, he'd be inviting you to be a partner with him and that washed-out-willie of a son of his."

"From what I hear, Sydney's become a good doctor."

"If he's not much of a man, what kind of a doctor can he be?" Miz Mac asked tartly. "At least Burleigh has a strong, definite personality, even if he does rub my fur the wrong way sometimes."

"But he's been here a very long time, and he has a lot of influence. How can we fight him?"

"The way most battles like this are fought—with money."

Rachel knew her aunt was right. She sighed. "Do you have any idea how *much* money we're talking about?"

"Half a million to start, maybe?" Miz Mac asked calmly.

Her eyes wide, Rachel nodded. "Yes, that would probably do for a start. But how in the world are we going to get that kind of money?"

Miz Mac hesitated for a moment, then said, "Your father and mother died suddenly, Rachel, with no chance to get their affairs in order. For some reason, maybe because you were young, your father never changed his will. I was his sole beneficiary, not you."

"But you always made sure I had every advantage," said Rachel softly.

"I sure tried," Miz Mac said, shaking her head, "but you were a proud, prickly little thing sometimes and wouldn't let me do what I wanted to."

"I didn't need to go to Europe, Aunt Lyddy," said Rachel, remembering the arguments they'd had about it. For once, she'd won.

"Be that as it may, your daddy left a sizable chunk. I always felt like that money was yours, not mine, no matter what the will said. I never touched it."

"Not even for my education?" But Rachel already knew the answer.

"Nope. It was my privilege, so don't say a word," she said fiercely, knowing she'd deliberately allowed Rachel to believe the money had come from her father's estate.

"Thank you, Aunt Lyddy," said Rachel humbly.

"No time for that. The issue at hand is, what are we going to do to stop Burleigh's plan to close this hospital?"

Rachel swung her legs for a moment. They didn't quite touch the floor, perched as she was on the high bed. She studied her aunt's face intently. "We've been together, just you and me, for a long time, Aunt Lyddy."

"Won't be just you and me much longer," she said with a little smile. "I'm pleased as Punch about you and Johnny. He's a good man."

"Yes, he is. But I know you well enough to know

there's something else on your mind. Come clean now." She caught and held her aunt's eyes.

"You do know me, Rachel. And there is something I've been thinking about. That hospital in Houston...well, they did a lot for me with all that fancy equipment, and Dr. Baker is as good a man as God makes. I know all that. But I feel...I feel...."

"Tell me, Aunt Lyddy, say it out loud."

She heaved a great sigh. "There's going to come a time when I'm going to have to face death and let it carry me off to Jesus, and Rachel, I'd just as soon be here, in this room or one of the others, as anyplace. I know I'm going to need medical care, and I don't want to be in that big hospital in Houston, no matter how technologically advanced it is. You understand, don't you?"

"I do. I really do." Rachel slipped off the bed and went to stand by Miz Mac's chair. "And there are others who feel the same way. It may be one of the best reasons for keeping this hospital open." At that instant she vowed she would. She'd find some way to do it.

For a couple of moments neither of them spoke. Rachel's hand was warm on her aunt's shoulder. Then, in a clear, pleased tone, Miz Mac said, "There is a balance of $436,784.92 in an account with your name on it in the Texas Commerce Bank in Houston."

Rachel's sharp intake of breath seemed very loud in the small room. "Four hundred thirty-six thousand, seven hundred and eighty-four dollars and..."

"Ninety-two cents. I made some good investments, Rachel. I had good advice. It's yours, all of it, to do with as you please."

"You know very well what I'll do with it," Rachel whispered. "You *know* what I'll do with that money!" Her voice had risen in excitement as she realized what might be possible.

"I have to admit the thought of the hospital crossed my mind." She glowered a little and added, "But the money's *yours*, and you're the one who decides what to do with it, understand?"

"Of course." Rachel's eyes had the shine of tears now. "Oh, Aunt Lyddy, we can—" She was interrupted by a knock at the door, followed by Nurse Patt's head sticking in.

"Johnny Cowboy on the phone for you, Doc, and your uh...friend is waiting for *you*, Miz Mac," she said with something very close to a leer. "If I don't watch it, you two'll have me running a dating service."

"Patt, I told you—"

Rachel left their banter behind as she flew to the phone, thinking it seemed like days since she'd seen Johnny instead of hours. "Johnny?"

"You win," he said softly. "I tried to wait until you called, but I couldn't. It seems like light years since I saw you."

"I was just thinking that."

"You sound breathless. Is this a bad time? Are you busy with a patient?" He paused and added, "Or does talking to me make you breathless, I hope?"

"I ran to the phone when Patt said it was you," she admitted. "There's a lot happening here this morning."

"Tell me about it," he prompted.

Rachel gave him a sketchy outline of Burleigh's plans, as well as Miz Mac's surprising announcement. "It looks as though we'll be able to make a good start, at least."

"That's a very impressive start, Doc," he said respectfully. "As I've said before, Burleigh's a creep, and your aunt is a special lady."

"Yes, she is." Rachel was suddenly aware of how very much she wanted to see him. "Johnny, I..."

"What is it?"

"I...when will I see you again?"

"You know I wish it were right now, for lunch, dinner, all night—I guess what I mean is forever! But—"

"But you're tied up all day," she said ruefully.

"You guessed it. There are some things in the wind around here."

"What kind of things?"

"I'll tell you when I'm sure. Think you can wait until this evening to see me?" His tone was light and teasing.

Rachel laughed. "No, I'm not sure I can!"

"Sounds to me as though you've got your hands full without me."

"I suppose." She sighed. "What time?"

"About seven, and dress in your best. We're going to celebrate. It's not every day a man gets to take his fiancée out for the first time."

"That sounds wonderful," said Rachel, not meaning plans for a celebration at all. His *fiancée*. What a pretty word it was. "I'll see you at seven." Rachel didn't want to hang up. "Johnny," she said softly, "I love you."

His voice was husky, a little lower than usual. "I told myself you did three hundred times on the way home last night, but it sounds so much better when you say it. I took a catnap before I came to work...and I dreamed about you."

"Good dreams?"

"Does the sun rise in the east?" He laughed. "I have *got* to get off this line or they'll fire me. And a man who's getting married..." He trailed off, as though he still couldn't believe it, then finally said, "A man who's getting married needs a job. Rachel, I love you, so much I want to tell everyone I see. But I'll just tell you again. I love you." He hung up then, not saying good-bye. Those three words were enough.

"Dr. McGeary? Are you in there?"

It was Nurse Patt, rhythmically waving her hands in front of Rachel's glazing eyes. "Oh, Patt, I'm sorry, I—"

"Don't be sorry. I'd give a Yankee dime to have that look in my eyes again!" She hugged Rachel, something she'd certainly never done before. "They want you."

"Who?" Rachel shook her head as if to clear it and

said apologetically, "Oh, you mean Aunt Lyddy and Stan."

"Yup, and from what I gather, it'll knock your socks off."

"Patt! have you been listening at the door again?"

She tried hard to look hurt. "Now Rachel, how can you say that?" With a grin she added, "Well, maybe a little."

What Stan Janek had to tell her was very good, indeed. "Dr. McGeary," he began, when the three of them were closeted in room 17, "Lydia has convinced me that I would regret not having a part in this little venture." His round face was made almost handsome by the smile he directed at Miz Mac.

"How much is she holding you up for?" asked Rachel, shaking her head at the look of insulted innocence on her aunt's face.

"I thought I'd start by matching the amount you have—"

"Matching it!" gasped Rachel.

"—and then go from there," he finished serenely. "I came from a little town a lot like Marvin."

He smiled at Lydia again, and she fidgeted with the raspberry cloche as though she might feel a sliver of shame at maneuvering him into helping.

"That's absolutely wonderful, Stan, if you're sure it's what you want to do," Rachel responded.

"I'm sure. I agree with Lydia. The medical center in Houston is tops. I'm certainly proof of that," he said simply. "But hospitals like this one are necessary, too. And this town is lucky to have a fine doctor like you who wants to work here."

"I...thank you, Stan, for...for..." Words failed Rachel, and her eyes filled with tears.

"We're the ones who ought to thank you. Now, I've got some plans to raise the rest of the money we'll need to start the foundation."

"The foundation?" echoed Rachel.

He nodded. "Best way to go. I'll get my people on it

right away, so you'll have a comprehensive presentation when you stand up before the board. You'll knock 'em dead, won't she Lydia? Come on, we've got things to do. The thing is, you have to introduce me around, so I meet who's who in Marvin. Get some fund-raising ideas sparking." He helped Miz Mac—who looked as satisfied as the proverbial cat who ate the canary—to her feet, and together they walked to the door.

"The trick is to involve the whole community as much as possible. Let 'em in on what's happening, especially what this Burleigh character is up to. And let 'em have a chance to help, to give their money. When people care about something they give their money." He added with that knowing, whimsical smile of his, "And they care about whatever their money is in."

He closed the door behind him, and Rachel wondered if he was aware of her need to be alone. He seemed to be a gentle, perceptive man, and she wished he had come into their lives a long time ago.

She went over and raised the blinds and let the bright sunshine in. It showed the peeling paint in the windowsill, the line of mildew that formed so easily in this damp country. There was so much to be done.

"And You've provided the means to begin," she whispered. "Oh, Lord, thank you for caring. I care, too, and I want to do what's right for my life." She was quiet for a very long time, in spirit and body. The assurance that came to her was as clear as though He'd spoken aloud, as though He'd said, "I've done My part, child. Now it's time for you to do yours."

"I will, Lord. I will! I'll give whatever I am, whatever You've made me, to this hospital, to making certain it continues. And...I thank you for Johnny, for his love!" She felt the bubble of happiness rise in her until she thought she'd burst. She took a deep breath, secure in the knowledge that God had prepared the way for the task ahead of them all. "If God be for us, who can be against us?" she whispered to herself.

Burleigh, for one, she answered silently.

Chapter Twelve

As the little community became more and more aware of the controversy, the lines were drawn, and inconceivable as it seemed to Rachel, one camp was solidly behind Burleigh. Stan Janek's shrewd thinking helped, for he kept saying that when it became common knowledge that the foundation wouldn't be included on the tax base, they would switch sides. It was Stan who coached Rachel tirelessly as she readied herself for the board meeting. Her days and nights seemed to be taken up with one phase or another of their efforts.

She did take time to tour the University of Houston campus with Dolly, who presented herself at Rachel's office one day. Dolly admitted that her father knew nothing of the trip and insisted Rachel keep it a secret, even from Deenie. Although it made her uneasy, Rachel agreed. Not even Johnny was aware of it.

To her chagrin Rachel found herself, more often than not, too busy to go out with him in the weeks that followed Burleigh's announcement. One night he overrode her protests and said he was coming out to see her anyway, after a rather late committee meeting.

She'd managed to rush home, take a bubble bath that wasn't nearly long enough to untie her aching neck muscles, and dress in a spectacular hostess gown of cherry red panne velvet. Miz Mac had bought it for her, saying it was a shame that blondes were always advised to wear cool, pale colors. As she surveyed her makeup, she saw her aunt had been right, as usual. *Red, at least this luscious cherry red, is good for this blonde*, she thought.

Johnny must have thought so, too, from the look on his face as he stood at the foot of the stairs. She came slowly down, feeling pretty, smelling pretty. He'd given her an extravagantly large bottle of Cabouchard perfume—a fragrance she hadn't worn before—which was exactly right for her. Its light, delicately sensual scent reached Johnny a moment before she did, and he came up the last four steps, not willing to wait until she reached him.

They stood on the stairs, her arms around his neck, her face lifted to his. He finally murmured, "If you looked any more beautiful or smelled any more heavenly, I might have heart failure."

"I wouldn't want that to happen; we haven't got the coronary care unit yet! Maybe I'd better go back upstairs—"

He caught her close. "If you think I'm going to let you go, think again." His hands moved slowly on the smooth satiny fabric covering her back. "Are you sure you want a Thanksgiving wedding? How about a middle of October wedding?"

Rachel thought... *It's October fourteenth.* "That sounds wonderful—"

"It sounds like you're both chomping at the bit," said Miz Mac from the living room. "Can't say as I blame you, but the invitations are printed, and the flowers all ordered. Sorry, you'll have to wait."

Johnny's arm was still around Rachel as they moved down the stairs. "Don't you have any pity at all?"

"Nope," she answered cheerfully. "I only have one wedding to plan, and I'm going to do it right even if you die from waiting, Johnny Allen!"

"I might," he said. "Doesn't she look pretty in that

color?" He touched her hair, which she'd left free.

Miz Mac's groan was more than a little theatrical. "I can't take much more of this." She went about halfway up the stairs and called down. "In case you two are hungry, there's some Pedernales River chili. I used Lady Bird Johnson's recipe, and it's good, if I do say so myself." When they didn't respond, she muttered a little, shook her head, and went on up.

The chili went uneaten. Johnny pulled Rachel close beside him on the sofa, and for a time neither was aware of much around them. Finally Johnny let her go and put his hands behind his head, eyes closed. "Rachel, I think about you at the office, when I'm in conference, when I'm home, in the car on the way home. I think about you all the time. And when we're together it's all I can do to persuade myself that we shouldn't..." He trailed off, opening his eyes now and looking down at her.

"I know." Just two quiet little words, but her whole self was in them.

"You really do, don't you? And you want me the same as I do you...just as much?"

"I do."

"My heart and my body tell me I can't wait, but my will tells me I can!" He caught her close again. "I really do love you enough to want the best for you. And I know the best is to follow His plan."

"I trust you, Johnny." She ran her fingers through his hair, loving the crisp, clean feel of it. "I'm just not always so sure I can trust myself!"

"Sweetheart, don't say that!" He hastened to add, "Oh, I like to hear it, but it makes me feel weak in the knees...weak, period."

"Johnny, I hope you know how much I'm looking forward to the time when we can express our love fully and know that's the way God intended things to be between a husband and his wife...."

"My wife." He gazed at her, awed at the phrase. "Rachel, we'd better go eat that chili, and you can tell me all about what's going on with the foundation and what's been happening at the hospital and—"

She met his gaze squarely. "I understand, and I'll try to help."

"Then you'd better start by putting a tow sack over your head and wearing your hospital greens all the time."

"You don't like my new outfit?" she asked, her warm gray eyes slanted up at him.

He hauled himself to his feet. "You little flirt, you know exactly what I meant."

She laughed, glad some of the tension was eased. "I'm starved. And Aunt Lyddy does make good chili." Hand in hand, secure in the knowledge that they could trust each other, they walked into the kitchen, the tantalizing aroma of Lady Bird's chili leading the way.

An hour later they stood companionably at the sink, Johnny leaning against the cabinets and watching as she put the pretty blue and white dishes into the dishwasher. "So you auctioned off an old caboose as one of the fund-raising projects?"

"Yes," said Rachel, her hands moving as surely and carefully with the delicate pink depression glass tumblers as they did in the operating room. "I thought it was one of Stan's better ideas"

"How much money did it bring?"

"Over thirty-five hundred dollars. A man who swears up and down he's going to write the Great American Novel is going to use it as his office. And thirty-five hundred, added to everything else, makes a respectable sum."

"Enough to persuade the board to keep the hospital open?"

"I think so," answered Rachel, suddenly serious. "Oh, I can't begin to think of losing."

"You won't lose." Their eyes caught and held, and he reached to the rack on the side of the cabinet for a clean white dish towel. With infinite tenderness he dried her hands, each finger in turn, placing kisses on their smooth tips, on her palms. "I'm going to go now, and I'm not going to kiss you good-bye," he said huskily. A glint of merriment lit his brown eyes. "And I'm going to take a cold shower as soon as I get home."

"Does it work?" Her voice was almost a whisper.

His grin was wide now. "Like you say at the hospital when they ask you how someone's doing, 'As well as can be expected!'" He did hug her once, hard, but he left without kissing her again.

Rachel had just fallen asleep when the phone on the bedside table rang. Knowing exactly where it was, she managed to bring the receiver to her ear without fully awakening. "Yes?" she murmured, then, more clearly, "Dr. McGeary speaking."

"Rachel, it's Johnny."

She didn't open her eyes yet, but she smiled. "You must have just gotten home. Have you been there long enough to take your shower yet?" she teased.

"There was a message on my machine from my dad."

Immediately alert, Rachel's eyes opened wide now.

He sounded subdued, almost hesitant. "He was mad, Rachel, really mad."

She knew, then. "Because I took Dolly around the U of H campus."

"Partly, but mostly because you didn't tell anybody. You certainly didn't mention it tonight."

The cool sound in his voice set her teeth on edge. "The main reason was that Dolly asked me not to. Another is, it didn't really concern you, Johnny."

"Of course it concerns me. She's my sister."

"Well, she's my friend. She asked for my help and advice, and I'm not the kind of person who says no to a friend."

"In this case it might have been better if you had. He's really mad, and I can't say I blame him."

Rachel felt the adrenalin begin to flow. "All I did was

introduce her to some people I know, who can help her. And by the way, why didn't your father call *me* instead of you, if he's so angry with me?"

There was a small deliberate pause before Johnny said slowly, carefully, "That isn't his way. He feels that since we're engaged, that you're going to be my—"

"Your woman?" supplied Rachel. "I'm beginning to get the picture. Jim Allen, the Big Thicket man, thinks his son ought to be able to control his woman better! That's it, isn't it?"

"I wouldn't put it like that, Rachel."

"Then how would you put it?" There was no mistaking her angry challenge.

"I guess I'd just say that when a woman doesn't use good judgment, it's up to her man to see that she does," he said bluntly.

"Johnny Allen! I've been responsible for my own actions for a long time now, and I don't need any man to—"

"Rachel, we're getting off the subject. We were talking about Dolly," he said, his voice showing the strain he felt.

"No, I don't think so. I think we've just begun to touch the real issue, which isn't my friendship with Dolly at all." She took a deep breath, trying to clear her head. She could hear their—hers and Johnny's—mockingbird singing its heart out from its favorite pecan tree. "We're right in the middle of our first argument, aren't we."

Gruffly he answered, "I guess we are. And the last thing I want to do with you is fight."

"Me, too." She changed the receiver to her other ear and began tentatively, "I suppose I should have insisted that Dolly tell Deenie she was coming to see me."

"I take it she approached you first?"

"Of course she did!" she retorted, feeling the stirring of anger again, quelling it with difficulty. "What did your dad tell you, that I slipped over to Saratoga and persuaded his daughter to sneak out and make horrible, illicit college inquiries?"

"Rachel, you've got a sharper tongue than I realized."

Almost meekly she said, "Isn't that what engagements are for, to find out about each other?" She was rewarded by his little bark of laughter.

"I guess so. Look, how about a compromise? At least check with Mama before you and Dolly go making any more plans."

"I can't do that."

"Why not? That seems reasonable to me."

"Because it's up to Dolly what and how much she confides in her parents, or you. But I promise I'll urge her to tell Deenie next time. You see the difference, don't you?"

"I'm not sure. All I know is, I'm tired."

Although she felt as though they hadn't really gotten to the heart of the matter, Rachel was touched by the weariness in his voice. "You need to get some rest. Things will look better in the morning. They always do."

"I suppose." After a slight hesitation he added, "I wish you were here with me now. If I could touch you, hold you in my arms, all this wouldn't matter."

She fought against her own sudden surge of desire. The image in her mind's eye was that look he got when he gazed down at her, when they kissed. Rachel was very much afraid he was right. The strong, mutual, sexual attraction they felt blurred the other facets of their relationship, made them fade and seem unimportant. And she knew they *were* important. "It isn't really very long until Thanksgiving, Johnny, and we need to use this time to...to know each other better."

"I know all I need to know."

"Johnny..."

"Get some sleep, Doc, and I'll call you tomorrow. Goodnight."

"Goodnight." She replaced the receiver gently, wondering why she felt so...so uneasy—so anxious, even. She got up and went to the window, grateful for the night air on her body. Papa Mockingbird was still singing. The sweet, fluid notes intensified the lonely, anxious feeling. Crossing her arms tightly over her breasts, she leaned against the window sash, searching the dark sky, fighting what her mind was whispering.

He's extravagant. He's impetuous. He's most likely very much like Jim Allen.... That stopped her. Was he, really? In a lot of ways he showed that he hadn't patterned himself after his father, but was he, deep down, of the same mind? Regardless of any of this, she longed so desperately for him it was a long time before she went back to her lonely bed, whose heart shape seemed to mock her. Someone had made that bed out of love, for love, and to lie down alone in it was something she was no longer content to do

On Thursday evening of that same week the conference room of the First State Bank of Marvin was crowded, and the discussion so far had been lively. Rachel glanced around the smoky room at the solid citizens who represented the town and who would decide the fate of Marvin Community Hospital. Burleigh was convincing, no question there. And each person in the room was listening carefully to him.

Burleigh was saying, "I realize statistics are hard to assimilate, but it'll help if you see them as I speak. Son, will you start these around for me?"

He beamed at Sydney, who, Rachel had to admit, did look as though he'd matured a good bit. She'd dressed carefully for the meeting, making certain she looked quietly, but not blatantly feminine in a soft suit of dusty blue with a cream silk blouse. She wore sensible shoes, and her hair was twisted almost severely on top of her head.

Young Burleigh lingered only a second longer than necessary as he handed Rachel a copy of the information she knew to be dismayingly true.

His father lowered his voice dramatically as he said, "You will notice that there is a substantial difference between the money taken in and operating expenses—wages and benefits of employees, supplies, maintenance, and so forth. Sirs, it is obvious that Marvin Community Hospital is, and has been for some time, operating in the red."

"Dr. Burleigh," spoke up the bank's president, Mr. Raider, "isn't that partly due to the fact that the hospital was built long enough ago that the current standards of the federal government were not considered?"

"Exactly true," purred Burleigh, the smile on his face small but satisfied, knowing that the more information brought out by the group and not by him, the better. "Even the doorways to the patients' rooms are substandard. Due to skyrocketing medical costs, we can no longer operate without government help in the form of Medicare and Medicaid." His eyes flickered to Rachel. "Dr. McGeary?"

"Yes?" she said, a little startled by his suddenly singling her out.

"What group would you say the heaviest portion of the patient load at the hospital is comprised of?"

"Why..." Rachel was aware the answer to that was going to help his cause, but she truthfully said, "The elderly and indigent, sir."

"Right," he said with a satisfied nod. "But surely you will agree that even if these people are poor and old, they still deserve topnotch medical care."

"Of course." By reminding herself it would be her turn soon, Rachel choked back the comments that rushed to her mind.

"Of course," he repeated. Now he turned his attention to the board. "Gentlemen, the hospital is not only substandard in construction, but it has also fallen into a state of disrepair, and there is no more money to bring it up to the level you and your families deserve. Why just recently a man died there, because of the lack of a coronary care unit."

He quieted the sudden buzz of conversation. Then with one quick triumphant glance at Rachel, he ended with, "And it is my understanding that Rachel McGeary, whom I value as the daughter of my esteemed, deceased colleague, recently delivered a woman in her home rather than use such deficient facilities. Dr. McGeary, I sympathize with you fully. Would you like to say something at this time?" He sat down, looking like a man who fully believes he's won the battle.

Rachel rose, grateful she'd prayed before coming to this meeting. She felt His presence now, and the thought calmed her, even dissipated the anger in her heart. "Dr. Burleigh, you haven't mentioned your proposed clinic." She saw the wary look spring into his eyes and took a gamble. "Wouldn't you like to take another moment to tell these gentlemen about it?"

"Why...of course," he said as he got to his feet again. "The reason I didn't bring it up was, um...well, because I feel this is a separate issue altogether."

"I don't see it that way, Dr. Burleigh." Rachel's tone was sweet, but definite. "Working together, your clinic and the hospital can make the medical service to our town what it should be, the best possible."

Clearly Burleigh was caught off guard. He'd expected her to denounce, perhaps even attack him and his plans for the clinic. "Ah...yes, Dr. McGeary, that's certainly what we want for the people here in Marvin. But while I'm preparing to build a clinic that will offer that, the facility that houses Marvin Community Hospital is not the best. Face it, Rachel, you have a sentimental attachment to it because your daddy built it!"

Rachel met his eyes squarely. "That simply isn't true, Dr. Burleigh."

"I contend that it is, and you can't face the fact that with the vast resources available at the medical centers in Houston, just thirty-eight miles away, we do not, I repeat, *do not need that hospital any longer!*" His hands were flat on the table before him, his body leaning toward her in his intensity.

Aware that the confrontation had narrowed to the two of them, Rachel said calmly, "Correction, Dr. Burleigh. *You* don't need that hospital any longer. But the people of Marvin do. And if I may, I'd like to explain why I helped Sandy birth her baby at home, instead of in the hospital. My reasons were far different from the one you've stated." She saw the interested, encouraging faces and proceeded to give a quick, comprehensive report, ending with, "Gentlemen, we must look with clear eyes at medicine and medical needs.

"I have to face the fact that the text books I slaved over during my education will probably be obsolete within ten years. Medicine is changing so fast that we as doctors can't begin to keep up with technology. But as important as technology is, it's more important that we physicians relearn that the care of the patient requires caring for the patient. To quote Sir William Osler, the father of bedside medicine, 'It is much more important to know what sort of patient has a disease, than what sort of disease a patient has.' And I propose that it is far easier to do that in a facility like our little hospital."

"Would you mind explaining yourself just a tad bit more, Dr. McGeary?" said a cigar-chewing, white-haired man.

Encouraged by his quiet interest, Rachel said, "People are expressing more and more their feelings of depersonalization in the huge medical facilities. Not that I don't admit the need, the blessing, even, of advanced technology." She thought briefly of Aunt Lyddy, who would have been lost to her months ago without it. "But I want to practice a different kind of medicine, in many ways the kind my father practiced here in Marvin Community Hospital when he was alive."

It was a calculated statement, but Rachel felt it was justified. Almost every man in the room remembered her father, remembered the countless times he'd served them and their families well. She continued, each word clear and precise, "I feel that the kind of medicine you need here in Marvin, the kind of medicine I want to practice, makes it an absolute necessity that we keep the hospital open." She waited, not looking at Burleigh as the buzz of conversation broke out again.

Finally Burleigh said, "I surely can't deny that some of your points are well taken, Rachel, darlin'."

So, we're back to that, and in front of everyone, she thought. But she merely smiled, biding her time.

"But the fact is, as usual, that it comes down to cold, hard facts...or cold, hard cash, which we are fresh out of," said Burleigh triumphantly as he sat down.

Rachel picked up the folder which Stan Janek had armed her with, though the facts and figures it held were burned into her brain. "Gentlemen, I have here several proposals." She went on to outline, briefly and concisely, Stan's plans for the foundation. "It would be made up of stockholders who made contributions of $100 or more, who will elect a board of twelve to fifteen members. They would meet yearly.

"One of those members will be selected to sit on a monthly quality assurance session, which will make certain we doctors are doing the best possible job. And one of us, as doctors, will be present at the foundation meetings. Not as a voting member, but so that each group knows what the other is doing."

Mr. Gilbert, the superintendent of schools, asked, "But Dr. McGeary, if the funds are depleted, how can we bridge the gap? I appreciate the efforts already made to raise money, but you'll have to admit the amount falls far short of what we need just to begin to refurbish the hospital."

"That's true," admitted Rachel, "but—"

"Give it up, Rachel," said Dr. Burleigh. His tone was kindly, patronizing. "You've given it your best shot, and we all appreciate what you've tried to do. Why, I'm constantly amazed at what a pretty little gal like you is able to do."

Rachel knew the anger that swept over her was wrong. She fought it. "If Dr. Burleigh could forget I'm a woman and think of me as a fellow physician—"

"Looking like she does, it'd be pretty near impossible to forget she's a woman, wouldn't you say? Can't imagine why she'd even want us to...." Burleigh's murmured words trailed off as he shrugged his broad shoulders.

Rachel's chin lifted a fraction. "Dr. Burleigh, members of the board, I have here a statement of the funds available, should you vote tonight to establish the foundation."

Expecting to see only the sums that had been publicly donated and raised to date, the men gratified Rachel by exclaiming in amazement at the figures. Satisfaction came as she saw Burleigh's stunned expression.

In answer to the sudden barrage of questions, Rachel answered, as she and Stan and Miz Mac had agreed, "The donors have asked that their names be withheld. But I think you'll agree that this amount will get us started well. I feel the town will be behind us and keep things going."

When the meeting finally broke up the matter was settled. A unanimous vote to establish the foundation was given on the first ballot. Even Burleigh, knowing he was beaten, had cast his vote in agreement.

As she drove home to share the news with Miz Mac she asked God to temper her pride. The one stipulation the board had made was that she continue to serve on staff at the hospital for at least one year. She'd said yes gladly, knowing it was right, that it was God's will for her. She laughed a little as the cranky little car zoomed toward home. It was possible she was happy enough to fly. Johnny would be so proud of her.... They'd won.

Chapter Thirteen

Johnny had given her the key to his apartment, though Rachel hadn't thought she would ever have occasion to use it. But every effort she'd made all day to reach him was futile. Evidently he'd had meetings scheduled at a conference center until late. So, after putting in a full day herself—word had gotten around about the board's decision and her part in it—she'd gone to his place to wait for him to come home.

She found some limes and a carton of Perrier in the refrigerator. There wasn't much else. Obviously Johnny ate out most of the time. She settled herself on the curved cream couch to watch the lights of Houston wink on. But her own lights must have gone out because the next thing she knew Johnny was sitting close beside her, his hand smoothing the hair from her forehead.

"Rachel, sweetheart, what are you doing here?"

She opened her eyes and looked straight into his warm brown ones. "I...I hope you don't mind, I let myself in...."

"Mind? That's why I gave you the key." He gathered her close and just held her for a while, letting her waken slowly. "I take it you felt the urge to visit."

She pulled away slightly. "Oh, Johnny, I have the best news!"

"Me, too, but you first," he said, kissing her nose.

"Well, the board meeting was last night, remember?"

"It was, wasn't it? I've been so involved in what's going down at the office the exact date slipped my mind. Tell me what happened."

Rachel felt a twinge of disappointment that he'd forgotten, but she was too pleased with her news to let it bother her for long. "They voted unanimously to begin at once on the foundation!"

"That's terrific!" He hugged her tight for a moment, then held her at arm's length. "Money really does talk, doesn't it?"

Quietly Rachel said, "I'd like to think the presentation Stan helped me with made a difference, too."

"Of course it did. Everything works together." His smile was delighted. "You did what you set out to do, keep the hospital open."

"It's not going to be easy, even with as good a beginning as we've made. The next year will tell the story."

"The next year..." he echoed. "Rachel, the next year is going to be the best in our lives."

"Yes, it will, won't it?" The look on his face was easy to read. She felt drawn to him almost irresistibly. Instead she shook her head, laughing a little. "Mmmm, no. Let's don't start!"

"And why not?" he teased, his fingers twining in her hair.

"You know exactly why not, because we can't finish it! Besides, you haven't told me your news." Eyes shining, pleased beyond measure because sharing good news with the man she loved seemed to be life's greatest pleasure at the moment, she watched him expectantly.

He looked dazed for a second. "Are you sure you don't have a tow sack to put over your head? It's hard for a man to think straight when he's looking at an angel."

"Try." It was her turn to ruffle his hair.

He caught her hand. "Rachel, we're going to Alaska!"

Her eyes widened with surprise. "You mean on a honeymoon?"

"That's not what I meant, but it's a good idea."

"Then what—"

"Our company is doing a lot of exploration up on the Kenai Peninsula—north of Fairbanks—and I've been offered a job as head geologist of the operation."

A tiny alarm went off in Rachel's mind. "And when would you leave?"

"*We'll* leave right after the wedding, but I have to fly up in a couple of days."

"This would be a permanent move?" There was no smile on her lips now.

"Sure, Doc. The job will last a couple of years, maybe more." He was silent for a moment as he saw the look on her face. Slowly he said, "You don't want to go."

"That's not it at all. In fact, I always thought I'd like it up there...as long as it wasn't on the frozen tundra, or whatever they call it."

He laughed a little, but his laughter had an uneasy sound. "As a matter of fact, we do have operations on the polar cap. But the Kenai Peninsula is close to the coast, and from what I hear, it's beautiful. Tall timber, mountains, post-card scenery, the last American frontier and all that."

"Sounds wonderful."

"But? There's something bothering you, Rachel."

She nodded. "Any other time I'd be delighted at the prospect."

"But not now." He leaned back on the curved sofa, his eyes serious and dark. "Out with it."

"Johnny, they've asked me to stay on at the hospital for at least a year."

"And you told them you would."

"Yes, I had no idea this would come up."

He nodded, his gaze thoughtful. "That's true, you didn't. But now that I've told you, and I know you'd like to go, you'll have to tell them you've changed your mind."

Rachel stared into his eyes. "I can't do that."

"Why not?"

"Because...because I committed myself."

He frowned. "I'm sure the board will understand, Rachel, and will release you from that commitment."

"They might," she agreed. "But whether they would or not is not the main issue."

"What *is* the main issue, then?" He stood up and walked a few steps away from the couch, then back, standing over her.

"Johnny, I had no idea you were even thinking of a move. If you'd told me, I might have made a different decision."

He took her arms and lifted her to her feet, then pulled her close. "Rachel, I know myself. I couldn't go up there alone, without you. Now that we've found each other and feel the way we do, I don't think it's best for us to have a long separation. You'll just have to trust my judgment, sweetheart. It's the best thing for us," he said softly.

She didn't have the strength to keep him from kissing her. When he drew away she wished with all her heart that she had. It made her next words all the harder. "But it's not necessarily what's best for me, don't you see? It's not just my commitment to the board, as important as that is. It's a promise I made to God, to make the very most of an opportunity I feel He gave to me!"

"But, honey, God wouldn't want you to go back on the commitment we've made to each other, either," he murmured against her hair.

"I...oh, I feel so—" She halted, unwilling to admit the depth of her confusion. She didn't want him to know just how weak she felt. Calmly, belying her inner state, she said, "Maybe we should let it go for a day or two, Johnny."

He eyed her keenly. "You know I'm right, that the decision for both of us should be mine. The head of the household is to have authority over those in his care, and they're bound to submit to that authority. It's biblical." He emphasized the last word carefully.

She felt as though she might explode, but she merely said, "Both of us have had busy days, and we're tired. We need to think about it for a while, and—"

"Thinking isn't going to change the way I feel about you, and it won't change what's right, Rachel."

She pulled away from his arms and the harsh sound in his words. He let her. She looked for her purse and put her shoes—which she'd slipped off earlier—back on. "I'm going home now. I...call me tomorrow?"

"I'm busy all day, but I'll come over tomorrow evening."

His polite, almost cool words cut Rachel to her soul. She walked to the door, wanting to say it would all work out, but she was not at all certain it could. "I'll see you tomorrow, then."

He nodded, making no move toward her, letting her go without another word or another touch.

The next evening Johnny got to Miz Mac's a good bit before Rachel did. He and Miz Mac had just finished the Texas equivalent of English high tea—barbeque beef sandwiches, German potato salad, watermelon pickles, and strawberry Bluebell ice cream. All but the pickles, which were Miz Mac's contribution, had been brought by Johnny.

"Johnny," she finally prompted, "would you like to talk about it?"

"Talk about what?" he asked, his smile too bright.

"Something's wrong between you and Rachel. I may be an old maid, but I've got eyes in my head. She's hurting." She sat on the love seat, her thin fingers clasping her iced tea glass.

Her last two words were like blows to Johnny and he

winced. "It's nothing we can't work out."

"You're sure about that?"

For the first time Johnny felt a flash of uncertainty. It showed in his face as he said gruffly, "I'm sure." He went on to explain what a wonderful opportunity the job would be for him, how he'd hoped for one like it. "Don't you see, Miz Mac, the most important thing is for a man to provide for his family in the best possible way he can. This would really be a step up for me."

She sipped delicately at her iced tea. "Yes, that's certainly true. But it seems to me you're forgetting that Rachel is a responsible adult too, with an important job she's fully committed to."

"I'm not asking her to give up being a doctor," said Johnny with a frown. He leaned toward her, elbows on his knees, hands dangling between. "A man would be a fool not to be proud of her."

As long as it fits in with his plans, she thought. "Johnny, can I ask a question?" At his nod she said, "When did you tell her about this Alaskan opportunity?"

"Last night."

"And when did *you* find out about it?"

He rubbed his chin thoughtfully. "Oh, I reckon it's been in the works for a month, maybe a little longer. Why?"

"It never occurred to you that you should tell Rachel sooner about the possibility?"

"No, I guess I wanted to surprise her."

Miz Mac wore a red bandanna on her head gypsy style tonight, and it made her look like a fortune teller about to impart a great revelation. "Johnny, Rachel's not some green girl who's going to walk three paces behind you."

Stung, he replied, "I never thought that!"

"Then why didn't you confide in her, ask her if what you wanted to do with your life—both your lives now, if you please—was what she wanted?"

He was frowning in earnest now. "I suppose I feel that it's up to me to make the decisions, and if she loves me, she'll trust me to make the right ones. It's not as though she couldn't practice medicine in Alaska. I'd venture to say the opportunities for a good doctor—and she's a good one—are even greater up there."

"I'm sure that's true."

He was on his feet now, pacing a little. Gracious as it was, the living room seemed too small to contain his feelings. "But what we do now is going to affect the whole tone of our marriage."

"Johnny, you haven't said truer words since you came tonight, with the exception that the potato salad was the best in the state," she said, trying to lighten the mood a little. "And I appreciate your wanting to start your marriage off right."

"Then you agree with me. You feel it's my place as the head of our family to decide what's best for us?" He stopped pacing and faced her.

Miz Mac was obviously thinking hard before she answered. "Not in the way you mean, Johnny."

"You don't?" The words fell like heavy stones in the quiet of the room. "But Miz Mac, it's *biblical*."

She chewed on her thumbnail, examined it, then chewed a moment longer. Finally she said, "I can see you believe that with all your heart. It's possible that what you believe is traditional, but not necessarily biblical, Johnny."

"I don't understand," he said slowly, his expression grave. "I've always thought—"

"Or have been taught," she murmured.

"Yes," he said almost angrily. "I was taught by my folks! Are you saying they taught me falsely?"

"I didn't mean to, Johnny. But I do feel we have to find our own way, our own answers from God, about His will for us in our lives. I'm sorry if it seemed like I was doubting the wisdom of your parents, or their integrity in training you. You're a fine man, and they obviously did a fine job raising you."

Johnny sat down opposite her, his eyes intent. "Whether you know it or not, you're suggesting that the way I've always been taught, the way I believe is right," he said doggedly, "isn't right at all."

She sighed. "The real test will come when you put it into practice in your relationship with Rachel, won't it."

His fine brows lowered, giving his face a serious, angry expression. "If this damages our relationship it will be because the world has warped Rachel's sense of what's right. All that women's lib stuff gets into their minds whether they want it to or not, and changes them."

Miz Mac knew there was a grain of truth in what he was saying, but it sounded very much as though he was parroting the words. Softly she said, "Son, a half-truth is the worst kind of lie—"

She was interrupted by the sound of the front door opening and closing and Rachel's light, hurrying step as she came through the entryway toward them.

"I'm sorry I'm so late," she said breathlessly, pausing to scan their faces. Her own was drawn and anxious as she came slowly into the room. "Johnny, have you been here long?"

"Long enough to have supper," said Johnny with a grave little smile. "There's plenty left." He waved a hand at the table which Miz Mac had set as elegantly as though they'd had watercress sandwiches instead of barbequed beef.

Rachel shook her head, the little tendrils of hair that always came down on a busy day flying out, then nestling close to her neck again. "No, I'm not hungry." Her eyes sought his, and her face grew even more anxious when she saw the look there.

Miz Mac got to her feet. "Well, I'll leave it here in case you change your mind. I'm going upstairs." Even as she spoke she was moving toward the door.

"You don't have to leave, Aunt Lyddy," protested Rachel.

"Oh, yes I do." At the arched doorway Miz Mac paused. "You two have the smarts between you to know what's right. Just remember, it takes His wisdom, too."

When she was gone it seemed very quiet in the room. Johnny was still on his feet, having gotten up when Miz Mac rose. His back was to Rachel, who sat huddled in one corner of the sofa. The seconds ticked by until she said, her voice small but clear, "It was hard leaving last night, with things unsettled the way they were. I didn't sleep much."

As he turned toward her Rachel saw that his eyes contained the same dark pain she felt. "Me neither."

At his gruff words, at the sight of the pain in his eyes, Rachel wanted to jump from the couch and fling herself into his arms. She wanted to tell him that whatever he wanted, she'd do. But something kept her silent.

Finally he came and sat beside her, not close enough to embrace her but close enough so that the light, lingering fragrance of Cabouchard reached him. He took a deep breath. "Rachel, I'm sure you know how important what we do now will be to our future together." She nodded wordlessly, her clear gray eyes meeting his. "No matter how many times I went over all this last night after you left, I came to the same conclusion."

"Me, too."

His eyes narrowed, and a small dent appeared between them. "This job in Alaska is an excellent career opportunity for me. You know that. It means a substantial raise in my salary."

"You make a lot of money already," said Rachel, knowing they were on the edge of something that had disturbed her for quite some time.

"That's true," he agreed. "And I intend to make more."

Rachel heard the veiled challenge in his words.

"There are things that are more important than money."

"People who have plenty, who've always had plenty, can say that a whole lot easier than those of us who haven't." There was a cutting edge to his voice now.

"I can't deny that. And you can't deny you're extravagant—"

"You certainly never protested when I spent money on you."

"Maybe that was *my* mistake," flared Rachel. "I know there were things I wanted to say but didn't, because I..."

When she faltered, he said carefully, "Why didn't you?"

"Because..." She trailed off, then began bravely again. "Maybe for the same reason you never mentioned you might be going to Alaska?"

"It's not the same thing at all," he protested. "Whether or not you like the way I spend my money isn't near as important as whether or not I have the right to make decisions concerning my life!"

Shocked to the core at his cold, hard tone, Rachel stared at him, then whispered, "Our life, Johnny, we're talking about *our* life!"

"No, we're talking about my job." They were no more than a couple of feet apart, but his words made it seem more like two miles.

"But don't you see, when two people decide to join lives, what each does affects the other profoundly."

"What I see is, that there's a principle involved here that is absolutely important."

"Which is?" Her voice was still no more than a whisper.

"Who makes the decisions, who has the authority in this relationship."

Rachel felt trapped. Not only by her commitment to the board of Marvin Community Hospital, but also by her lack of real understanding of the situation that confronted them. She couldn't actually refute his statements, for she felt there was truth in them. But neither could she wholly accept them. So she said the only clear thing in her head. "I can't go back on my commitment to the hospital. It's right for me. I know it."

"I have to be in Fairbanks day after tomorrow if I'm going to take the job." She was silent, and though his eyes willed her to relent, she said nothing. "Rachel, our relationship will only deteriorate if I'm up there for long periods at a time, and you're down here. You know it can't progress, develop naturally, if we're apart."

"That's probably true."

"I can't marry you and leave you here."

Rachel felt her heart stop but found the strength to say, "Then maybe we should..." She started to say postpone, then lifted her chin and said, "Call off the wedding."

"Is that what you want?" he asked fiercely.

"It might be for the best."

There was a terrible intensity in his eyes now. He moved a little nearer and gripped her shoulders. "I'm not the kind of man who begs, Rachel."

"I wouldn't want you to. But we have to face the possibility that we've... that we've made a mistake," she finished shakily. Her eyes, however, were steady and looked straight into his.

"I don't think so," he said vehemently. "Rachel, if I could prove I'm right by the Scriptures, would you change your mind?"

Rachel had no idea how much time elapsed between his question and her answer. "Don't ask me again, please. I *can't* change my mind, not and still look myself in the eye! Surely you understand that."

He let her go and stood abruptly. "I understand one thing, that you don't care about me as much as I thought."

"But I do!"

His look was thoughtful. "I'll be gone for the next few weeks."

"The next few weeks?" Their wedding date was only weeks away.

He chewed at the side of his mouth for a second. "You're thinking about the wedding, aren't you?" She nodded, and he said, "You might be right, when you say we ought to call it off. At least until we straighten this out."

"I'm not sure we can, Johnny."

"Rachel, how can you ignore the fact that God Himself set things up the way I say? How can you?" When she said nothing, just stared helplessly at him, he repeated what he'd said earlier, prompted vaguely in part by Miz Mac's statement that he ought to form his own conclusions. "I'll study the Scriptures and show you...."

The tears were so close now they made Rachel's eyes shine. "I'm really tired. Maybe we've talked about it long enough. Maybe there aren't any answers....Maybe we're just wrong for each other after all!" Suddenly she couldn't bear being in the same room with him a moment longer with things the way they were. She ran blindly past him and up the stairs, leaving him standing in the room alone, the frustrated anger on his face.

It wasn't until he heard the slam of her door that he shook his head a little, then slowly walked to the front door and let himself out.

In the days that followed Johnny didn't call, not even before he left for Fairbanks. Rachel was grateful for the steadily increasing flow of patients in her office. Some had trivial problems, and some were more challenging, like Lana Beth, who was doing well. Rachel was becoming aware of how easy, at least in some ways, it would be to settle into the life of a small-town doctor...a single doctor. The days were fine. They were busy and interesting. But when she had to go into her quiet room with its mocking heart-shaped bed, she slept badly. She went through stacks of medical journals, even raided Miz Mac's small horde of historical romances. And she was delighted when, a couple of weeks after Johnny had left, Deenie called and invited her to visit.

After she hung up the phone, Rachel stood staring out the French doors in the breakfast room for a long time, until Miz Mac came up behind her.

"Girl, it's no crime to admit you miss him."

Rachel turned to face her aunt, the tears spilling over. "Oh, I do! But I'm not sure anymore about things...."

"Who was that on the phone?"

"His mother. She invited me up to Saratoga to visit. Aunt Lyddy, she said the nicest thing, that it makes her heart feel easier to be around me." Rachel didn't mention something else Deenie had said. Dolly and Jim had had quite a "ruckus." She thought grimly that she knew what about and hoped for Dolly's sake—and Deenie's—it had blown over.

"Looks like they've all taken a shine to you."

A wan smile curved Rachel's lips. "I don't think that includes Johnny's dad. He thinks I'm a modern, liberated female who's leading his women astray."

The merry blue eyes twinkled. "And are you?"

"Sort of, I guess." She heaved a huge sigh. "What are your plans for tomorrow?"

"Now, Rachel, you've got to stop planning your life around me. I can take care of myself." She put her hands on her hips. "You do so well with your patients. But when it comes to me—"

"When it comes to you, it hurts too much!" The words fairly burst from Rachel's lips.

"I know." She fiddled with the red bandanna on her well shaped head. The scarf had become a favorite. "But I feel that this...illness might be the greatest challenge I've ever faced, or ever will. It means that whatever I do, I'll enjoy it the very most I can, that I can savor every good gift God gives me, appreciate it, even

163

more because...well, because we ought to anyway."

There was no fear in the blue eyes. Rachel honestly didn't remember ever having seen any there, except maybe once when she'd been in an accident and they'd called Miz Mac to come to the emergency room. With a little shock she realized that not once had she and Johnny spoken of the time she and Aunt Lyddy might have left together. There was no way of knowing how much, how long. "Aunt Lyddy, you really should meet Deenie Allen."

"Why's that?"

"For more reasons than you can shake a stick at! Deenie has some wonderful old pieces that I'm sure you'll like. And...and I'd just like for the two of you to meet." Her last words were convincing, for they were absolutely true. She could see the idea was appealing to Miz Mac.

"You know, I just might enjoy a trip to the Thicket. Been forever since I was there. Call Miz Allen and see if it's okay."

Delighted, Rachel hugged her. "Oh, it'll be fun! I can't imagine why I never thought of taking you before."

Dryly Miz Mac muttered, "As cuckoo as you've been about that good-looking man, it's a wonder you can remember how to put one foot in front of the other and walk."

Rachel laughed, feeling better than she had since ...since that good-looking man had left. She told herself she could face even Jim Allen tomorrow, eyeball to eyeball, and not be intimidated.

Chapter Fourteen

As it turned out the next day, Rachel had to do just that—face Jim Allen—because he answered the door. In the flurry of introductions that followed Jim managed to convey quite clearly that he wanted to speak to Rachel alone. Though Deenie frowned and Miz Mac looked fierce, Rachel accepted his firm invitation to ride down to the service station where he worked to pick up a part for the vintage car he was restoring.

Though it was a few days into November, the air bore only a hint of coolness. However, there'd been a kiss of frost earlier, and some of the moss-hung sweet gum trees flared as proudly crimson as any New England maple. The ride was spent mostly in silence, until he parked under an ancient spreading oak tree adjacent to the station. Jim made no move to get out, and he glanced over at her a couple of times, as though he was trying to decide exactly what he wanted to say.

Rachel had made up her mind to let him speak first. She had no illusions of being able to persuade him to change his attitudes or views. She only hoped to respond in such a way that he wouldn't be antagonized.

Finally he said, "I can't make out like I'm not relieved that Johnny and you've called things off."

"I understand."

"Do you understand how much you've turned things

upside down in my family?"

She cringed at the blunt question. "Oh, Mr. Allen, I certainly never meant to do that."

The sincerity in her tone took him back a moment, but he said, "I don't reckon you did, but that's not the point. Just being the kind of woman you are is what did it."

"I can't very well help being what I am, can I?"

"No," he admitted slowly, "I guess not. The world and all affects young people before they know it."

"You're talking about Dolly now, aren't you."

His nod was vigorous. "The other night she came clean of the whole scheme her and her mama cooked up, the playhouse, the savings account, the whole thing."

"I see."

Angry now, he riveted his hard gaze on her. "Do you, really? Do you see how hard it is for a man to realize his wife has been going behind his back?"

"Mr. Allen, this began long before I came," Rachel said, and she rushed on before she lost her nerve. "And as for my taking Dolly around the campus, I...I'd do it again."

His scowl was eloquent. "You've got no right to mess in our family's business."

Knowing she might regret it, Rachel said, "It's you who have no right to impose your will on two people whom I'm sure you love very much."

"Of course I love them. That's why I try and protect them, to take care of them!"

"But you can't take care of Dolly forever, don't you see? She has to learn to take care of herself, to make decisions for herself." When he didn't answer Rachel pressed what she felt was an advantage. "She's bright, and if you trust her, she'll do fine. Think of how painful it is for parents who, because their children will never mature for some reason, have to take care of them all their lives. It's a great burden, even if it is a burden of love."

He sighed and rubbed a hand over his eyes. "When you put it like that, I'm not sure about things. But one thing I'm certain sure of."

"What's that?" Rachel asked softly, realizing that Jim Allen, like everyone else, had hidden weaknesses.

"The other night Dolly stood up to me with fire in her eyes and told me if I didn't say it was okay for her to go to college, she'd marry Joe Bob Connor next week." His eyes were pained and angry at the same time now. "Sajd he'd already asked her seven times, that he was—"

Quickly, before he could say anything more about the hapless Joe Bob, Rachel said, "What did you tell her?"

"What could I say? She's like me in a lot of ways, one of which is that she don't make idle threats. When I say something, you can count on it."

"I'm sure that's true," Rachel murmured.

"Anyhow, I told her I'd think on it, and she said there was no time for that. She had to get her schedule all planned out."

"And?" Rachel was holding her breath. Even at eighteen Dolly was wise enough to know that if her father didn't agree to her going to college it would make a great deal of trouble between her parents.

Jim's scowl deepened. "I told her if she had her head set that hard on college, to go on."

And you didn't want her marrying Joe Bob, thought Rachel. "Mr. Allen, all this was bound to happen sooner or later. Surely you know that." The sun shining through the windshield was warm on Rachel's knees, even beneath the denim skirt she wore.

"I suppose, but it was you who stirred things up." Suddenly his deep brown eyes caught and held hers. "You and Johnny going to patch it up between you?"

Caught off guard, she stammered. "Why...I, I don't

know if we can...if we can work things out."

"I won't lie. I always thought Johnny deserved a woman like my Deenie, hoped he'd be as lucky as I was and find one. But if he still wanted you, I wouldn't stand in the way of your marrying," he said stolidly. "He's a grown man and will have to abide by his choice."

Eyes wide, feeling an amazing variety of emotions at his attitude toward her, Rachel could only say, "I don't know what's going to happen."

He opened the pickup door. "I'll only be a couple of minutes. You wait here for me. Want some soda water?" When she shook her head, he shrugged, then got out, slamming the door behind him.

Rachel latched onto the one positive sort of statement he'd made....I won't stand in the way of your marrying if Johnny still wants you. *If Johnny still wants me*. She shivered in spite of the warmth, because she wasn't at all sure he did.

It was no surprise to find on their return that Deenie and Dolly and Miz Mac were already well on their way to being friends. The three were in Deenie's playhouse, which clearly delighted Miz Mac.

Dolly was telling her about the beautiful split oak baskets adorning the low beams. "Miz Blaine, over at Honey Island, makes them. She's one of the few around who still remember the old ways of doing it."

Miz Mac scrutinized the graceful, curved basket in her hands, admired its sturdy construction. "These would be wonderful in my shop. I'd sure like to meet this Miz Blaine."

"Would you?" Dolly's smile was as bright as the late morning sunshine that streamed into the small-paned windows and lit up the homey, beautiful little room. "I'll be glad to take you over there. She can talk the horns off a brass billy goat, though."

Laughing, her mother said, "That's the gospel truth,

but she's a good old soul. You two go on. I'd like to talk to Rachel."

"Have a good time, Aunt Lyddy," said Rachel, thinking that after her talk with Jim, a session with Deenie couldn't be too bad.

"I'll see to it!" said Dolly, tugging at Miz Mac's arm.

Rachel watched them leave, thinking it wasn't every girl Dolly's age who would willingly, even gladly, spend time with women so much older than herself. She said as much to Deenie, who nodded in agreement.

"She's a good girl. I was really afraid for her when she stood up to her daddy the other night."

"I'm glad he agreed." Rachel, seated at the little table opposite her, reached over and put a hand over hers. "Deenie, I'm sorry about my part in things. It seems as though I've been nothing but trouble for you."

Deenie's eyes kindled. "That's not true at all! If it hadn't been for you, me and Dolly might still be planning and hoping. And now, she's going to be starting school—with Jim's permission—and I don't have to sneak around anymore. Why, things are a hundred percent better since Johnny first brought you here, Rachel."

The mention of Johnny's name made her throat tight, but Rachel smiled anyway. "You can't tell me it wasn't too wet to plow, as Aunt Lyddy would say, around here for a while."

"You got that right. Jim ranted and raved his full allotment. He had it coming," she hastened to add.

"It was Dolly herself who made the difference."

Soberly Deenie nodded. "I have to tell you it scared me silly when she said she'd marry Joe Bob. I knew she wasn't bluffing, and he's crazy about her. He'd have taken her off in a minute."

"Poor Joe Bob." The young man's homely face flitted through Rachel's mind.

"I feel bad for him, too. But it wouldn't have worked out. Dolly would always have been yearning for something more than he could give her."

In the little silence that followed, Deenie looked steadily into Rachel's clear gray eyes and saw the sadness lurking deep in them. "Rachel, what about you and our Johnny?"

Rachel met Deenie's gaze as long as she could. Then, she got up and moved restlessly around the room, touching a pretty dish, looking closely at a carefully stitched quilt. Finally she stood at the window, hoping the peaceful view would calm her. "I love Johnny, Deenie. I...I even think I may love him like you did Jim when you first met."

Deenie's laugh was low and delighted. "Honey, God Himself gave me the love I have for Jim. If He gave it to you for Johnny, then it'd be a crying shame for you to let *anything* stand in the way of you two being together."

"It's not that easy!" burst out Rachel. "Just loving each other isn't enough."

"Why not?" Deenie listened quietly, calmly, as Rachel tried to explain about her commitment to the hospital, about how she felt she couldn't go back on it. "And what about your promise to marry my son?"

"Deenie, he issued what amounted to an ultimatum! He said it was up to him, as the head of our family, to make decisions, to say what's best for us." When Deenie looked as though she thought that was perfectly reasonable, Rachel added, feeling slightly reckless, "To tell the truth, it sounded more like Thicket philosophy than Bible doctrine."

"Could be. But, Rachel, he's not altogether wrong. Someone has to take charge, take on the responsibility. And I can't help but believe it's the natural order of things for a man to do it. The world would be a better place if more men realized that."

Rachel hesitated, not wanting to further risk the easy communication between them. "Deenie, can I ask you something very personal?"

"Of course."

"Do you ever get tired of having Jim always make decisions for you? Choosing your furniture, your clothes, shaping your days, even?"

It was a long time before Deenie spoke. Her voice was low, and each word seemed to come from somewhere deep within her. "Yes, I can't deny it. Sometimes I do. But I weigh things a lot, Rachel, ponder them in my mind. And the bedrock truth is, a long time ago I made one decision that affects everything now."

Rachel knew what she meant. "When you decided to marry Jim."

Deenie nodded. "I may have been green as a gourd and young, but I could see what kind of man he was. A man who needed to be in charge, who believed it was his God-given responsibility to act in a way laid down by generations before him."

"I see." Rachel was beginning to understand the depth of the convictions that Johnny had voiced. The realization was not comforting.

"Rachel, the decision I made way back then affects what I do now. I chose to marry Jim Allen, and the main thing to me now and always is that my marriage to him endures."

Regardless of what it costs you personally, thought Rachel. "It's really too bad more people today don't feel that way about their marriages."

"That's for sure. What about you, Rachel? Can you tell me you feel that way about Johnny? How far are you willing to go?"

Frowning, Rachel said, "Deenie, things are not so simple or clear cut. I made a commitment to stay at the hospital, and that's very important to me."

"Is it more important than the one you made to Johnny?"

Feeling as though a heavy weight was resting on her chest, Rachel found she couldn't speak. Finally, her voice thick with tears, she said, "I don't know how to answer you, except to say that I love your son, so much there've been times, late at night mostly, that I wondered if I'd die from it!" Shakily she tried to laugh, but it turned into a wracking sob.

Deenie got up and came over, put her arms around her. "I know, I know," was all she said. She held Rachel's shaking body until it quieted. "Just seek His will. Be sure it's *His* will, whatever you do."

"I want to. But, Deenie, it's hard to *know* His will."

"What you need is a cup of Jim's coffee. It'll put hair on your chest. At least he says it will." At Rachel's hiccupping little laugh she said, "Don't worry, I've been drinking it for almost thirty years, and I'm not the least bit hairy! Come on inside to my kitchen, Rachel. As you told me, it's pretty fine."

Their eyes met, and Rachel was suddenly aware that Deenie Allen was the kind of woman every girl hoped to have for a mother-in-law. Hesitantly, she said so.

"That's an awful nice thing to say...." Now Deenie's eyes glistened. "I once read that a woman decided daughter-in-law didn't exactly say what she felt about her son's wife and changed it."

"To what?" asked Rachel.

"Daughter-in-love," was the soft reply. "Rachel, I'd be pleased to have you for my daughter-in-love."

Rachel hugged her tight. "You're right. I need some of Jim's coffee. He and I had a talk too, and I think we got things straight, at least mostly." Her arm still around Deenie's waist, the two of them went into the house.

Dolly and Miz Mac came in later and joined Deenie and Rachel at the table in the kitchen. The admiration in Dolly's eyes was obvious as she handed Miz Mac a cup of coffee. "You should have seen her, Mama, dickering with Miz Blaine."

"I was fair," protested Miz Mac, admiring the lovely old rose-sprigged cup as she took a sip of the Louisiana coffee, a dark roast laced with chicory. "Strong enough to make you want to slap your grandmaw," she muttered. "Did you hear the story about the man from over Opelousas way? He said they make their coffee in a bell, and when the clapper stands up, it's ready!"

Her parodied Louisiana accent made cawfee out of coffee, bay-ul out of bell. Everyone laughed, including Rachel. But her heart hurt at the thought of how very much the Allens, even Jim, had come to mean to her, and how well Aunt Lyddy fit in with them. *It would all be so perfect if only... if only Johnny and I can make it right....*

The four women were still laughing, sitting around the table, when Jim came in scowling and said, "It's lunch time."

Wickedly, Miz Mac said, "It sure is. What are you fixing for us today, Mr. Allen?"

His eyes widened, but Deenie got up and went to him, her arm about his waist. "She's teasing you, Jim Allen. I've got some beef stew all ready to heat up. Won't take a minute. You sit down there and charm Miz Mac."

Looking as though he'd rather charm a den of rattlers, Jim sat down. In spite of himself, by the time Deenie put an excellent meal on the table, Miz Mac had *him* charmed. It seemed Jim Allen liked jokes as well as she did. They were all laughing, Jim the loudest, as they clasped outstretched hands for him to ask the blessing.

At that particular moment she missed Johnny so badly she felt a physical pain... very near her heart. Her physician's mind had difficulty with that most unscientific fact.

Miz Mac decided they'd make a loop, going to Beaumont and then home, rather than retrace their route through Hardin. Rachel set a leisurely pace as she drove up Old Bragg Road, trying to block from her mind that night she and Johnny had parked there.

Because of low slopes and impervious materials within or below the soils, most of the Big Thicket is poorly drained. The resulting wide marshy areas and slow-moving creeks and bayous make the dense growth thick and forbidding. The palmetto spikes, low-hanging gray Spanish moss, the innumerable variety of growing things formed a tangle that suited Rachel's state of mind.

"They're really fine people, aren't they?" said Rachel finally.

"Sure are," was the laconic reply.

Silence again, making Rachel realize it was up to her. Aunt Lyddy wasn't one to force a confidence. "I don't know what I'm going to say to Johnny when...if I see him again."

"Oh, you will. Did you and Deenie talk about it?" Her blue eyes were shrewd. At Rachel's slow nod, she asked, "And what did she tell you?"

"That...oh, pretty much that Johnny's right, I guess," she said heavily. "And I do respect her judgment."

"She's a fine woman, and you could do worse than patterning yourself after her. But Rachel, I think there's something that we've skirted around but never really nailed down."

"What, Aunt Lyddy?"

"Submission, and what it really means." She glanced over at her niece. "The word doesn't mean something good to you, does it? Come on, tell the truth."

"I...no," said Rachel honestly. Johnny's words came to her. *It's biblical, Rachel*. She knew that even though he hadn't actually said the word, submission was what he'd meant. "I'll have to admit it makes me uneasy to think of submission. It sort of means having someone lord it over you, dominate you. No, it doesn't have good associations."

"That's really too bad. Submission, as God intends it, is a good thing."

"Tell me how, Aunt Lyddy."

Miz Mac was silent for a half mile or so before she said, "My understanding of it isn't perfect, I know. But I have studied the matter in the Scriptures, and I've asked God to give me light on it."

When she halted, Rachel prompted, "And?"

"Well, you've heard me say more than once that God will give you knowledge of His word if you ask."

"Aunt Lyddy," said Rachel, "you're stalling!"

She chuckled. "Maybe I was, a little. But I know what I have to tell you might sort of go against what Deenie and Johnny and that handsome rapscallion Jim Allen might say was right."

"Say it anyway," urged Rachel.

A little smile twitched Miz Mac's mouth. "I believe submission doesn't have to do mainly with a man and his woman."

"I don't understand."

"And no wonder. The world has a way of putting the em*pha*sis on the wrong syl*la*ble," she said. "But where you start is with a person—man or woman, all the same—and their submissive relationship with God."

"Oh," said Rachel thoughtfully. Somehow the idea of submitting to God didn't seem bad at all.

"You're beginning to see." Miz Mac's tone was satisfied. "What's important is that we submit our will to Him every day, each of us. Then it isn't hard to submit to each other."

"I never heard it put like that."

"Pity. Most of the time when the word comes up these days it's so some man can dominate some woman and do it by the Scriptures."

"Aunt Lyddy! You sound awfully cynical."

A tiny look of guilt flitted over her thin face. "I guess I do. I'll work on that. But think about it, Rachel. If you had a husband who, first thing every day, submitted to his God, wouldn't you trust him, want to follow him to the other side of China?"

"Yes, I believe I would," she answered softly.

"The trick is, you have to do the same thing yourself. I'm convinced that's the way it's supposed to work." Her grin was mischievous as she added, "It's like the childless woman who thinks she has all the answers to

175

raising kids. Only I'm an old maid who knows all about being married!"

Rachel reached over and clasped her hand. "Married or not, you have the answers. When I think of it like that, submission is a beautiful word, like...like love."

"I've always thought love means putting the person you care about ahead of yourself, thinking of them first. If two people do that, how can they keep from building something good?"

"Oh, Aunt Lyddy, I hope I get the chance to try." The words hung in the air. Neither said much as they came to the edge of the Thicket, then after a few miles, to the outskirts of Beaumont. "Do you still want to go into Beaumont?" she asked.

The tone of her aunt's voice as she answered told Rachel how exhausting the day had been. "No, let's go on home. I'd like a cup of that new tea and a nap."

Desperately Rachel searched in her mind for the words to pray. The only thing that came was... *Give me grace, Lord.*

It was perhaps a week later that Rachel, her heart heavy, broached the subject of the wedding to Miz Mac. "I'm sorry I haven't brought it up until now," she said apologetically over breakfast one morning. "But we really have to do something about the wedding arrangements." Her eyes met Miz Mac's keen blue ones for a long painful moment.

Miz Mac began gathering up the dishes. "Heard from Johnny lately?"

As bad as she felt, Rachel couldn't keep from laughing. "You know I got a letter yesterday!"

"And you know I never asked what was in it, either, even if I did almost pop!" Her laughter mingled with Rachel's for a few brief seconds. "Girl, you haven't been laughing much lately. It's good to hear." Mischievously she added, "What did he say?"

The laughter faded from Rachel's eyes. They became

as bleak as the gray November sky outside. "He said he's been doing a lot of thinking, and...and he was wrong about something." She rose and took a clean cup towel from the second drawer.

But as she picked up one of the tumblers, her aunt said, "Rachel, how many times have I told you, let God dry those dishes. If you do, it gets lint all over 'em. Besides, you hate to dry dishes. You're just putting off telling me what Johnny said. Out with it."

Her voice low, Rachel said, "He told me, before he left, that he felt it would be wrong for him to be up there without me."

"And now?"

"Now he says it was the best thing he could have done, that he...he actually is glad to be away from me."

"Pshaw, you must have read the thing wrong! I can't believe he said that—"

"But he did." Suddenly she flung the cup towel down on the counter. "Aunt Lyddy, I'm sorry, but I have to get to the hospital."

"What's your hurry?"

"Dr. Burleigh has as much as said he won't be bringing many more patients to the hospital here. Something to do with the mess there, or so he says." Work to bring the building up to code had already begun, and Rachel had to admit it really was a mess. "And did I tell you he tried to hire Patt to work in his new office?"

"He didn't!"

"He did." Rachel polished the counter absently. "Thank goodness she refused his indecently good offer. I'd hate to think of working without her. Aunt Lyddy—"

"What, honey?"

"If you wouldn't mind, if it isn't too much trouble, would you please take care of the arrangements to cancel everything? I don't know if I can." Her chin was lifted even higher than usual.

"I'll take care of it," Miz Mac promised, her face troubled.

Misery in her eyes, Rachel said, "Do you think I ought to give in, tell him I'll resign and go up there with him?"

"Don't ask me that, Rachel."

"I am asking you!" Rachel pressed her knuckles tightly to her mouth, aware she was being unreasonable.

Miz Mac picked up the cup towel Rachel had flung down, snapped it smartly, and folded it. "Almost everything in me says absolutely not. But—"

"But what, Aunt Lyddy?" asked Rachel.

"I've had a good life, Rachel, and with you a part of it, I've had almost everything a woman could want."

"Everything but the love of a man." Rachel knew the story of Miz Mac's lost love. Everyone in Marvin knew, at least bits and pieces. "Tell me about him." A look of such sadness flitted across her aunt's face that Rachel was filled with remorse. "I shouldn't have asked. Forgive me—"

"No, no." A crooked little smile lit her face. "I'd like to tell you. Sit down and I'll make a fresh pot. I always wondered why you never asked before. Didn't you say you had to get to the hospital?"

"I've got time," said Rachel, taking her place at the table again. These days each moment she spent with her aunt seemed infinitely precious. "Was he handsome?"

That little smile still curved Lydia McGeary's mouth. "I certainly thought so. Tall, with brown hair and the most beautiful brown eyes...a lot like Johnny's. But he wasn't much like Johnny any other way. He was quiet, a thoughtful man who didn't sparkle much, unless...."

"Unless he was with you," supplied Rachel softly.

Miz Mac nodded. She sat opposite Rachel, and for a moment the only sound in the room was the bubbling of the coffeemaker. "They never even called it a war. The Korean Conflict. But he went off for his tour of duty. Only a year, they said."

"His name was Andrew, wasn't it?"

"Yes. You know, even now, after all these years I can't say his name without a little pain, right here." She pressed beneath her left breast. "We decided to wait until he got back to marry. And we both pledged to keep ourselves for the other. Only he never came back. Missing, they said at first, then, a prisoner of...of conflict? And they were never really able to tell me exactly what happened to him."

"That's terrible." Rachel whispered.

"It was. His mother never got over it. And I waited and waited, until the months faded into years. Finally, when your parents were killed and you became my...my little girl, it seemed enough." She added quickly, "Rachel, almost always you were enough."

"I understand."

"And if Johnny's not the right man, there'll be someone better," said Miz Mac, obviously ready to put her memories back where they'd lain for so long.

"I have my work—" Her aunt's keen gaze stopped her, but she stubbornly added, "It's important to me, too, and I'd better go."

"Yes, you'd better." Miz Mac's tone sounded normal, but there was a certain look in her eyes.

Rachel went to her and stood close. "Thank you for telling me about Andrew." She bent and hugged her tight. "Thank you," she whispered again. *For so many things I could never name them all...* "I'll be home early this evening."

"I'll be here, girl."

As she went out to face a busy day, Rachel refused to give space in her mind to the question... *For how much longer...?*

Chapter Fifteen

Even with her busy schedule, memories of Johnny were never far from Rachel's thought. The two of them at Galveston in the fresh Gulf breeze...their first kiss; the sweet darkness of the Thicket all around them, his arms around her; the deep, husky voice at sunrise...when he'd said he wanted to watch all his sunrises with her.

The sound of his voice. She yearned to hear it so badly that one evening when the phone rang and she did hear it, she was hardly able to speak. "*Johnny?*"

"Yes, Doc, it's me. What's wrong?"

She cleared her throat. "Nothing, nothing. I must be coming down with a cold."

"Hey, don't do that. In a whole month in the wild Alaskan wilderness, I never caught one. And I'm coming home."

"You're coming home?"

"I sure am, be there tomorrow evening." He hesitated a couple of moments, then asked softly, "Have you missed me?"

It wasn't in Rachel to lie or be coy. "Yes, Johnny, I have."

"You know we've got to talk."

"I know." She twisted the phone cord, leaning against the elegantly turned mahogany spindles of the staircase.

180

She'd been on her way up to her room when the phone rang. Years of self-discipline imposed upon her by schooling, medical training—and Aunt Lyddy—made her say, "Johnny, I haven't changed my mind about... about anything."

"Does that mean you don't want to see me?"

"It...might be better if we didn't—"

"Do you still love me?"

She closed her eyes, glad he couldn't see her face. Why did it have to hurt so badly? "Yes, I do."

"My flight is a late one. I get into Houston Intercontinental at 6:02."

"Do you want me to pick you up?"

"No, I need to go to the apartment first and make some calls. Is eight o'clock okay, not too late?"

"No, it's not too late." Even as she said it, the little voice in her mind said, *Are you so sure?*

By eight o'clock the next evening Rachel had changed clothes three times. She'd finally settled on the red panne velvet gown Aunt Lyddy had bought for her, mainly because the bright color bolstered her courage. When she heard a knock at the door and glanced at the stately old walnut grandfather clock, she saw that Johnny was exactly on time. As she swung open the door her heart didn't beat faster. It seemed instead to slow down, to synchronize itself with the clock's dignified chimes.

He stood looking down at her, and she could see he'd dressed carefully. His rich chestnut leather jacket cropped at the waist, the cream turtleneck sweater, and the dark brown cords made him look even more wonderful than she remembered. Rachel stepped aside, realizing they'd been standing in the chilly November air for several moments. "I'm sorry. Here I stand like an idiot, and it's cold! Come on in, you must think I'm—"

"I think you're the most beautiful sight I've ever seen," he said, his voice low and his eyes dark. She closed the door behind him, and they walked into the living room. He didn't touch her, but he added, "And I've seen some spectacularly beautiful sights in the past few weeks. You can't believe how beautiful it is up there until you've seen it."

He headed straight for the fire burning in the wide grate, his hands outstretched. Then he turned to face her, his expression open as always, but curiously, not revealing much. Rachel smiled brightly. "You liked it, then?"

"Very much. It was the strangest thing. When I got my first glimpse of the mountains and a lungful of that clean, cold air, I had the feeling it was something I'd been looking for all my life." He went on, enthusiastically describing the countryside.

The more he talked, the more Rachel realized it wasn't just his job that was the center of attraction. The north country itself had already gotten into his blood. When she ventured a comment to that effect, he grinned and admitted she was absolutely right. With a little lift of her chin she said, "I'm really glad you like it. Are you hungry? Aunt Lyddy left a pot of something for us."

"She's not here?" Rachel shook her head, and he said, "Thought we needed some privacy, I take it. Well, we do, and no, I'm not hungry, except just to look at you some more." He hadn't sat down, though she had. He came now and dropped beside her on the couch, his purpose plain in his eyes.

"Johnny, please don't." Rachel's strangled protest stopped him, but he didn't move away. The question in his eyes made her say slowly, "It'll only make things harder if you—"

"If I kiss you? I'll take that chance." He bent his head and touched her lips gently, tentatively, with his. At her shiver of response he caught her close. "Rachel, these weeks without you have been so bad, and so good, I didn't know if I'd live through them!"

She laughed, a breathy little chuckle against the smooth leather of his jacket. "That requires an explanation."

He drew back, kissed the tip of her nose once, then moved to the far end of the couch. "You're right about one thing. It's easier to talk when there's distance between us. If I'm close enough to kiss you, I will. Rachel, there was plenty of work for me up there but also a lot of time for thinking about things—you and me in particular."

Rachel met his eyes. "Before you go any further, I—"

"I know. You told me on the phone. You haven't changed your mind, and I respect the way you stuck to what you believed was right."

"Aunt Lyddy said she'd take care of cancelling all the arrangements—"

"I know," he said again. "I talked to her."

"You did? She never mentioned it to me."

"I asked her not to. Rachel, you're the only woman I want, the only one I've ever wanted." He grinned wryly. "When I told you I was studying the Bible a lot while I was up there, that's sure the truth. Among other things I read the part about the gift of celibacy and decided God hadn't given it to me!"

"Johnny!"

His grin broadened. "Well, He didn't. Rachel, look me straight in the eye and tell me you don't believe He meant us for each other. Can you?" he demanded.

She stared into his brown eyes. "No, I can't. I've never felt the way I do about you, not ever. And...and I don't think I ever will about any man again. But, Johnny, you said it yourself, there has to be more than feelings."

"I know. Commitment, for instance, right? And before I left I never really took yours as seriously as I should have, certainly not as seriously as I did my own." At the look on her face he said, "I can see you agree."

Suddenly she felt trapped, as though it was useless to

talk about the situation any more, useless and very painful. "There's no point in going all over that again. Please, let's don't take a chance on hurting each other any more."

"I hope I don't ever hurt you again," he said softly.

"Then let's just eat supper, and you tell me about your job, and let's don't talk about...about—"

"Our future?"

She nodded. "It's hopeless, Johnny. We have to face it sooner or later, and better sooner, don't you think?" She pleaded with her eyes for him to agree.

But he shook his head. "Rachel, I'm really sorry."

"For what?"

"Oh, mostly for playing the macho Thicket man. It's a wonder I didn't try and pull you off to Alaska by that beautiful head of hair."

"Ouch." Something hopeful stirred in Rachel. She listened expectantly, waiting for his next words.

"For another, it was wrong of me not to tell you about the job being in the works, because if I had, things might have turned out differently. I'm not making excuses for myself, but I got used to doing what only concerned me. I made my own decisions. Can you see that?"

"Yes, I can," Rachel murmured.

"There weren't many entertainment opportunities up there, hon, and I did read a lot. Miz Mac sent me some interesting Scriptures to look up."

"She did? Just how much have you two been in touch, anyway? It seems as though she heard from you more than I did." Rachel tried to sound accusing, but somehow the fact that Aunt Lyddy and Johnny were on such familiar terms made her feel grateful instead of left out.

"Could be." Johnny stared at the fire for a long moment, then said soberly, "Before I left I never even thought about how important the next year will probably be for you...and her."

He didn't say it might be their last, just as Rachel couldn't even say it in her heart. But she was deeply touched that though she'd never brought it up, Johnny realized it. "Yes," she said slowly, "it will be very important, especially to me."

"She means a lot to me now, too. I never met anybody quite like her. I've always read my Bible every day, or tried to, but usually a few Proverbs or a Psalm, sometimes the gospels. But she ah...strongly suggested I study Ephesians 5:21, not just 5:22."

"What does it say?"

He grinned. "Verse 22 says, 'Wives, submit yourselves unto your own husbands, as unto the Lord.' "

Rachel raised an eyebrow. "And verse 21?"

" 'Submitting yourselves one to another in the fear of God.' "

"I see," said Rachel thoughtfully. She felt that little surge of hope again.

"Honey, I went up there with every intention of finding absolute proof, straight from the Bible, that what I believed was right."

"*Was* right?" she questioned. "You've changed your mind?"

"Yes, I have." The grin was gone, and his face was serious, even grave. "Being the head of a family doesn't mean quite what I thought it did. In fact, I discovered when I read the whole book of Ephesians that God expects me to care for you the same way Christ does for His Bride."

"The church," Rachel said softly.

"That is one heavy thought, isn't it? And I realized that if I really loved you—and I do, Rachel—I had to grow up and learn how a real man of God makes decisions. That those decisions had to be made according to what's right for *us*. Not just me, or you, but us." He slid a little nearer, near enough to take both her hands in his. "Your hands are cold."

"Yes." It was all she could get out. Her mind was

filled with the question, *What does all this mean?*

Johnny rubbed her small cold fingers gently. "I told my boss that Bill Partlow, the young man who went up with me to look things over, could handle it for the next year, if I go up occasionally. I'll have to work just as hard on the project here, but I won't be living up there."

"Johnny, what are you trying to tell me?"

"That I'll be in Houston until a year from this January, as things stand now."

"*You turned the job down?*"

"Sort of."

"How can you sort of turn a job down?"

"Well, if that hot-shot young geologist Partlow gets much smarter, he'll steal my job while I'm down here. He was delighted to get the chance to take my place."

"Oh, Johnny...." It was what she wanted, but somehow Rachel felt sad.

It must have showed on her face for he said, "Look, Doc, more than likely things will go according to plan and we can both move up there next year. But if not, if old Bill's light shines bright enough and I miss out on this one, it'll be fine."

"How can you say that? I can tell you love it up there already!"

"I do." He moved closer yet. "But I love you more, and I honestly believe if we don't get to go to Alaska on this job, God will make a better opportunity for me."

She stared into his eyes, so close to her own. "Johnny, you're different somehow."

"You mean it actually shows?" His expression was a sweet mix of humility, pleasure, and something she'd seen before—the look of love she felt in her own heart.

"Oh, yes, it shows." She took her hands from his warm grasp and placed one on either side of his face, brought it close, and kissed his mouth.

"Rachel," he murmured against her lips, "Rachel, you'll let me cherish you, you'll marry me?"

"You know I will," she breathed.

The fire burned low, and the lights in the room were dim. Johnny finally said, "When the thought first occurred to me that it wasn't right for me to take the job now, I also thought of how the guys in the office would bait me, say I was letting myself be led around by the nose by a little bitty female."

She saw the glint in his eyes. "And you don't think they'll say that?"

He chuckled. "They'll say it, all right. But we'll know the truth, won't we?" Suddenly he asked, concern replacing confidence, "You don't think changing my mind shows weakness, do you?"

"Johnny, if a friend had told me her man made the decision you have, I'd be very, very impressed," she said softly. "But since you're my...you're going to be my husband, I'm absolutely awed."

"Hold that thought." He kissed her temple, felt the steady beat of her heart there. Mischievously he added, "And if you could show a little awe for me when we're around my dad, I'd appreciate it. He's going to say I'm starting out all wrong—"

"And with the wrong woman," murmured Rachel, her lips against the smooth skin of his forehead as he stroked her hair.

"But we know better." He pulled the pins, one at a time, and slowly ran his fingers through the wavy golden stuff. "Next Thursday we're getting married." The awe was in his voice, now.

She drew away. "But Johnny, it's all been called off!"

"Oh, no, it hasn't. Miz Mac agreed to go ahead, and she hasn't called off anything. She said if I couldn't talk you into it, she'd do it the day of the wedding if she had to. And that's just six days away."

"I can't possibly get ready. I haven't got a dress—"

"Do you want to marry me?" He was suddenly very serious.

"You know I do!"

"Then let's go ahead as we planned. I need you, Rachel," he said huskily. "And there's no reason for us to wait now. Besides, there'll be a lot of people at the church, and we can't disappoint them, can we?"

She took a deep breath. "No, we can't, can we?"

"Now, let me kiss you, oh, fourteen more times, and then let's have supper. I'm starved."

"Fourteen?"

"Fifteen," he said, sneaking a quick kiss to her throat.

"Fourteen more," Rachel said, laughing, her arms tight around his neck. "Fourteen more."

Along about kiss number twelve, Johnny sighed into the fragrance of her tumbled hair, reached into his pocket and withdrew a wide, pinkish-gold wedding band. As he slipped it on her finger, he answered the question in her eyes. "It belonged to my grandmother, whose hands must have been as small as yours. Mama wants you to have it, if it suits you."

Tears blurred her eyes as she held her hand up. "I love it...and I love her! If only— "

"You're thinking about my dad, aren't you?" She nodded. "Don't worry, he'll come around." Johnny grinned and added, "He's not stupid, just hardheaded, and he's a good man."

"I know." She traced the outline of the smooth gold circle and said, "I suppose you want this back?"

"How about if you trade it for the three kisses I've got coming?" he asked, already pulling her to him.

"It's just two...or maybe it is three!" She laughed and gave him the ring, the kisses, her life; knowing there would always be precious little she wouldn't gladly give Johnny Allen, ever.

Forever Romances are inspirational romances designed to bring you a joyful, heart-lifting reading experience. If you would like more information about joining our Forever Romance book series, please write to us:

> Guideposts Customer Service
> 39 Seminary Hill Road
> Carmel, NY 10512

Forever Romances are chosen by the same staff that prepares *Guideposts,* a monthly magazine filled with true stories of people's adventures in faith. *Guideposts* is not sold on the newsstand. It's available by subscription only. And subscribing is easy. Write to the address above and you can begin reading *Guideposts* soon. When you subscribe, each month you can count on receiving exciting new evidence of God's Presence, His Guidance and His limitless love for all of us.